MANY
SHADES OF
BLUE

LEE DEROCHE

MANY SHADES OF BLUE

iUniverse books may be ordered through booksellers or by contacting:

iUniverse
1663 Liberty Drive
Bloomington, IN 47403
www.iuniverse.com
1-800-Authors (1-800-288-4677)

ISBN: 978-1-5320-7287-1 (sc)
ISBN: 978-1-5320-7288-8 (e)

Library of Congress Control Number: 2019909550

Print information available on the last page.

iUniverse rev. date: 07/12/19

Acknowledgments

My thanks to the Hutchinson Center at the University of Maine in Belfast, Maine. Without the writing classes offered there this project would not have come to fruition.

Many thanks to my dear daughter, Karen Flemion, who found much of my source material, released in 2018 by the National Military Archives.

My warm thoughts toward many friends at Penobscot Shores, who encouraged me and shared stories of their lives to spur me on.

Last but not least, to my best friend, lover, and pilot husband, Tom, whose twenty-eight years of flying experience has piloted me though this book as well as our fifty-five years of marriage.

To Joanna, Birgitta, Betty, Jane, Chandler, Cathy, and Carolyn W.,
who started me on my journey

This is a story of a Maine family and the many truths and untruths that dominated their lives through many years. It begins with the story of the precocious Libby as she seeks truth about the circumstances that surrounded her birth and an uncle who she never knew existed.

The reader will be transported from 1960 in Skowhegan, Maine, back to World War II in 1944, where an American pilot was shot down over France and eluded capture by the Germans with help of the French Resistance.

He received the Caterpillar Club award from the manufacturer of the silk parachute that saved his life and the Flying Boot decoration for his walk to freedom into Spain. Much of this story is factual with documentation, released in 2018, by the National Bureau of Archives in Washington, DC.

The villages described in this novel are the actual places that were part of this American pilot's story. The handwritten account, documented in his 1944 debriefing conducted by military intelligence in Britain, is the basis of this book.

Many of the stories are based on actual tales that I was told while growing up. Some of the characters are fictitious, but others are easily recognizable to those of us who know them well and love them.

CONTENTS

Chapter 1   Blue Haven 1

Chapter 2   Blue Velvet 4

Chapter 3   Blue Cocoon 10

Chapter 4   Waiting Game Blues 13

Chapter 5   Bluebird Flight 15

Chapter 6   Boston and Beyond...17

Chapter 7   Blue Horizon 20

Chapter 8   Blue Heaven... 26

Chapter 9   Blue Challenge... 30

Chapter 10 Blue Haze 34

Chapter 11 Blue Moon... 38

Chapter 12 Blue Dawn... 42

Chapter 13 Way to Pau 44

Chapter 14 Bleu Soleil.. 47

Chapter 15 Blue Smoke 50

Chapter 16 Lavender Blue 54

Chapter 17 Blue Mist... 57

Chapter 18 Blue Twilight 60

Chapter 19 Blue Chateau 63

Chapter 20 Lapis Blue.. 66

Chapter 21 Goodbye Blues... 69

Chapter 22 Little Blue and White Lies 71

Chapter 23 Blue Mariposa.. 73

Chapter 24 Blue Bus to Pamplona 77

Chapter 25 Gran Hotel Le Perla 80

Chapter 26 Blue Future 83

Chapter 27 Blue Waters of San Sebastian 86

Chapter 28 Blue Atlantic 88

Chapter 29 Blue Oceans Merging 91

Chapter 30 British Blues 93

Chapter 31 Red, White, and Blue Future 96

Chapter 32 Blue Lightning over San Antonio 98

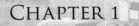

CHAPTER 1

BLUE HAVEN

November 1960

Wind-blown fog from the Kennebec River created surreal ghostlike images around the gingerbread trim on the old Victorian houses along Riverside Drive in Skowhegan, Maine.

The usual dog walkers passed by, intent on exercise for themselves and their furry charges, and they took no notice of autumn leaves that swirled and fell to the ground in anticipation of a more robust breeze. Early-morning activities, including deliveries of newspapers and dairy products, were right on schedule to provide news and nutrition to families hungry for both. Blue Haven Funeral Parlor was on the list of recipients of these services.

The Carlow family, proprietors of this facility, was now the second-generation keeper of the flame of the care of the dead. Leo, the patriarch of this family, inherited the business from his uncle. Leo's wife, Emm, was invited in when she married Leo. Their children, Libby and Len, were welcomed into the fold upon their birth by these loving parents. This happy family of four lived upstairs over Blue Haven in a rather large and luxurious family dwelling. The day-to-day operation of a funeral home was more of a lifestyle than a job that one went to each day. There was a practical advantage in living close to the dead.

Each day was different from the one before. Even though the phone rang constantly, Leo, the consummate professional, met the needs of his bereaved clients with compassion and respect.

This particular Monday morning found the family in the kitchen. Emm cooked breakfast, Leo read his paper, and the children argued over possession of the last dregs of milk for their cereal.

Libby stated emphatically that Mr. Rusty, their milkman, would be outside about now with their daily delivery of the dairy order. She jumped up from the table and announced, "I'll go down and get the milk, and maybe when I come back, Len will have stopped chewing with his mouth open with food falling everywhere. He makes me gag."

"I hate your guts, Libby!" Len replied.

"Now, children, let's be civil!" was Leo's standard comment when his children were being unruly. He continued to read his paper, seemingly uninterested in anything else.

Libby left the room and slammed the door behind her, driving home her anger. She paused at the top of the stairs and looked at her reflection in the large hall mirror. She liked the way the sun danced off her red hair and created a halo around her head. She was not a vain girl, but like any sixteen-year-old, she needed validation of her personal appearance and never passed by a mirror without checking her image. She used to ask Emm why she looked so different from the others in the family. Her brother and parents were tall and long-boned with dark hair and eyes, while she was petite, blue-eyed, and had curly red hair.

Emm always answered, "'Tis the luck of the Irish, my sweet girl."

No matter, Libby liked the way she looked.

Libby swooped down the long mahogany staircase and pretended to be a beautiful movie star. She swung open the heavy Lalique door and stepped outside into the cold morning air. She looked down and noticed the dairy truck parked near the curb. Off to the side, she saw Mr. Rusty lying faceup with his cap skewed over his ear. A set of false teeth sat next to a wire basket that contained milk and eggs.

"Mr. Rusty, are you dead?" Libby said. Having seen many dead people at Blue Haven, she embarrassed herself by asking such a dumb question, even though there was no one to hear. She stood for a moment and collected her thoughts. She thought of her father's words that "death is inevitable and comes to all of us." Still, this was different; it was someone she knew. She grabbed the wire basket and raced upstairs with the news.

"What took you so long?" asked Emm. "We are waiting for the milk."

"I was gone so long because I was making sure that Rusty is dead."

Now everyone was riveted on Libby.

Leo leaped up from the table, went out the door, and was down the staircase in three strides. He yelled back to Emm, "Keep the kids up here, and you drive them to school today!"

The school bus was the usual mode of transportation, but a bus full of school kids that would stop here in the middle of this might not be good.

Leo knew instantly that Mr. Rusty was dead but checked his eyelids—fixed and dilated—and found no palpable carotid pulse. As Leo's assessment continued, Officer Flagg appeared around the corner on his usual neighborhood rounds. Not being very particular about his professional demeanor, Flagg adjusted his drooping uniform pants and wiped chewing tobacco drool from his lip. Officer Flagg proclaimed, "He's toast, Leo."

"Thanks for your astute observation, Flagg! Stay here a minute while I bring the wagon around. You can help me load him in."

"No can do. I gotta bad back, and the union says no liftin'," Flagg said.

"Whatever you say! Onderdonk will be here soon to finish up the work left from yesterday. He'll help me." Leo picked up the false teeth, tucked them into the dead man's pocket, folded the milkman's cap neatly, and tucked it under the white belt of his crisp white uniform.

As if on cue, a 1957 silver Corvette Stingray roared down the street and screeched to a stop in front of Blue Haven. Andrew J. Onderdonk, MD, Somerset County's infamous medical examiner and forensic pathologist stepped out on the curb. He was quite a vision, dressed in his signature blue scrubs, blue Roper boots, and a blue Stetson hat.

"AJ, what are the odds on this milkman finishing his rounds today?" asked Leo.

"Well, now, zero and none! The SOB looks deader than shit!" proclaimed Onderdonk. "Let's load him in the wagon and put him in the cooler. Wow, my lucky day! I can hone my skills!

The two men placed the milkman on a stretcher and transported him into the morgue and into a locker beside another client who waited for forensic services.

Just another day at Blue Haven—your full-service mortuary.

CHAPTER 2

BLUE VELVET

Eight o'clock the next morning found Libby filled with dread at the thought of going down the front steps to catch the school bus. She took a deep breath and walked carefully on the opposite side from where Mr. Rusty had fallen. But the picture of him lying there, with his false teeth popped out of his mouth, was ingrained in her memory.

"Oh well," she whispered softly. "He died doing what he loved—delivering milk to children!"

She climbed onto the bus, but the strap on her backpack fetched up on the door handle, jerked her backward, and caused her to fall against the bus door.

"What you got in there, darlin' that's causin' you such a ruckus?" asked Mrs. Cyr, the bus driver.

"Just the usual stuff: books, gym clothes, snacks, and my lunch," Libby answered.

"What happened to the milkman at your house yesterday? Did he stub his toe? Rusty always rushed around—serves him right for not payin' attention!" Mrs. Cyr had never been known for her compassion.

"Nosy old bag! None of her business anyway," Libby whispered quietly as she wrangled herself into a seat while the school bus started with a series of small jerks before resuming the route.

Never one to waste her time, Libby reviewed her Latin declensions and prepared for a quiz today. "Amo, amas, amat … veni, vidi, vici … enough already! I will ace this quiz!" She pressed her face against the cold glass windowpane of the bus.

***

The bus screeched to a halt in front of L'École de Sacre Bleu just as the last bell rang. Libby bounded up the granite steps, burst into the classroom, slid into the seat of her desk, and folded her hands in anticipation of prayer.

Prayers today would be demanded by Sister Mary of Perpetual Help. The nun looked exceptionally mean as she walked around the room tapping her ruler on each desk as she passed by. The nun made eye contact with each student, and each student gave her a quick glance and looked down quickly. Libby never looked away first, forcing the nun to acquiesce or stand there for an uncomfortable length of time while the class giggled.

Libby's knuckles were swollen, sore, and painful when she clasped her hands in a state of grace. Sister Mary was a firm believer in converting left-handed students to the more conventional use of the right hand. The use of the left hand for writing, no doubt, was the work of the devil. Therefore, in the nun's mind, the devil lived in Libby, according to church doctrine. Ruler smacks, inflicted on the left hand, would drive the devil out, and the right hand would dominate. So far, Libby had proved to be a challenge for the frustrated nun. Libby got through the day unscathed.

***

Three o'clock, last bell, and off to music lessons. Emm was outside waiting for Libby, and the two drove off to the Bassega Brothers Studio.

Libby jumped out of the car and shouted, "See you later, Mum!"

Libby loved playing her accordion. The music connected her with her mother's side of the family, even though they all lived in Poland—and she had never met them. She opened the closet door where her instrument was kept and pulled it out onto her lap. The vintage, baffled mother-of-pearl beast was kept at the music studio since it was too cumbersome to juggle back and forth from home to the studio.

"Welcome, our dear Elizabeth!" It was the usual greeting from the Bassega twins. "Today, we request that you play our favorite song 'Roll Out the Barrel' for us, and we will work on your hand positioning on the keyboard."

Never the shy student, Libby answered, "I've played that song forty eleven thousand times. How about something new to inspire me? Do you have some sheet music?"

If the truth was known, the Bassega twins couldn't read a note of music, but this was a carefully guarded secret.

"Oh, Libby, you know how we love it when you play our favorite polka. Just play it in a different tempo, like a fox-trot!"

"What's that anyway, a type of dance? I'll just play your polka then!" She sighed.

Libby struggled to please her music mentors. As they asked her to spread her legs wider and wider, the pleats in her skirt allowed the accordion to drop lower and lower, thus the inner sides of her thighs were exposed. Their creepy stares went unnoticed by Libby as she gave her best musical rendition of their favorite song.

Music lesson over for the week and then back home for snacks to assuage her appetite until dinner.

Libby needed comfort. A recent renovation of one of the family reception rooms provided her with a space for quiet introspection. Even though her favorite place was inside the blue velvet-lined display coffin, she knew her size was becoming an issue. She had always been very slim, but her increasing height was beginning to prevent her from disappearing into the lace and folds of her surroundings.

She entered the heavy silence of the repose room and curled up on the blue velvet love seat in front of the fish tank at the far end of the room. She became mesmerized as she watched the light glow eerily in the tank. Tiny jets of water bubbled upward. Fish greedily fought for food. They rocketed to the surface of the water, gulped their feast, and sank to the safety of the bottom of the tank. Snails sucked and slithered on the inside of the tank and left a silvery track on the glass, unaware of the survival of the fittest that went on around them.

Even as a young woman at a vulnerable stage in her life, Libby recognized the significance of this life balance that would always affect her life.

Libby was cold on the love seat and missed the warm velvet comfort of the display coffin. She left the busy world of fish and snails and climbed into the coffin. She felt the familiar softness of her blue hiding place. Her Barbie dolls were just as she had left them, and they smiled and rested against the inside of their blue velvet prison. At sixteen, Libby still delighted in the company of her dolls and snuggled with them as she became relaxed and happy.

In her dreamlike state, she heard muffled voices coming from Leo's office. Dr. Onderdonk was there dealing with details from the previous day. She listened. The passion in the medical examiner's voice was hard to ignore. He and her dad were having a meeting of the minds.

"Andy, we do not need to open heads for a forensic exam, right?" asked Leo.

"Not sure, Leo. It is my responsibility to give these families cause of death and closure. This is how I see it. We unzipped the milkman yesterday and saw a ruptured aorta—no-brainer! Minimal bleed of scalp on occipital prominence. The guy croaked before he hit the steps as result of a ruptured aorta—end of story! No need to open his head!

"Now, the chick in the cooler from two days ago is different altogether. No sign of foul play, no bruising, and the Y-cut revealed no injury. She is as pure as the driven snow. We must open her head, Leo. Therein lies the malfeasance," concluded the pathologist.

Leo shrugged and sighed. He hated the sound of the scalp being peeled back from the skull and the circular saw as it screeched and bored into the head. The bits of bone and tissue that were launched everywhere made a mess, and the smell was acrid. He hated doing heads!

"Get out the Canada mints, Leo. We're going in!" AJ Onderdonk had the last word.

With that said, they delved into the mission before them.

The two colleagues chatted during postmortem exams. The small talk made the time pass quickly.

Leo started the conversation. "Emm and I have discussed this, and I know this is short notice, but any chance that you would be available full-time here over the next week or so? I want you to run the shop here, along with Emm, while I am away for a bit. Emm can handle the day-to-day stuff, but we need you for the messy stuff."

"Sure, what's going on with you anyway? A mortician convention teaching you guys how to screw more money out of the bereaved?" Andy asked. He was deep into his work and only half-heartedly listening to Leo.

Leo said, "I am going to Texas to visit family—but not just for the hell of it. The fact of the matter is that my brother John has the IRS breathing down his neck over his finances concerning his mortuary business. He owes the feds big bucks and thinks maybe I can help him sort through his dilemma. Anyway, I want to take Libby along with me. We can have a father-daughter trip while we renew family ties with my brother and his family. As you know, Libby will graduate in June and is off to college next fall. This may be a good time for a father-daughter trip. We'll fly into San Antonio and take a hop to Del Rio, near the Mexican border, where John will pick us up."

"You can count on me to bail you out, Leo, old boy. Hold that thought! I must interrupt this soap opera! Just as I suspected, the cause of her untimely demise was an aneurysm of the basilar artery! Weakness in the arterial wall caused ballooning of blood vessels and, henceforth, the rupture of the vertebral arteries as well. It's likely a congenital thing. Now, don't you feel better knowing the cause of her death? Jesus, I'm a smart son of a bitch! You're so lucky to have me instead of some new guy who might frig around all day and never figure it out! Now, what were you saying about the Texas trip?"

Leo continued, "In addition to the aforementioned reason for travel, my younger brother, Earle, will be joining us on the flight. John, Earle, and I have always looked out for one another ever since we were parceled out among relatives after our mother died. Our father didn't want to be saddled with young kids, so the three of us were farmed out to our mother's relatives during the Depression. Lib has known nothing about Earle since he was the black sheep of the family. His past indiscretions during WWII didn't sit well with our puritan New England family. Even though he was a decorated pilot and somewhat of a maverick hero, he fell out of favor with some relatives.

Andy became more engaged in the conversation. "Christ, Leo. People don't give a shit about that kind of crap anymore! This is 1960! Your brother should have been welcomed back with open arms. They were all heroes and should have been thanked for their sacrifice! Let's clean up this mess, and you can tell me more!"

With that conversation over for now, their subject was placed in a cold storage locker alongside Mr. Rusty. The two corpses were now ready for the journey through Blue Haven.

***

Emm and her staff would honor the corpses by making sure that they were dressed in their Sunday best. This project would be carried out before rigor mortis locked bodily joints in eternal stiffness. Hair would be expertly coiffed, and makeup would be applied with a heavy hand in an effort to make the dead seem less dead. Sentimental objects loved by the deceased would be placed in the coffin alongside the loved ones. This act of thoughtfulness more often assuaged guilt felt by family and friends than to provide any real purpose other than to clutter the viewing field.

Private time for the family, visitation, funeral services, and burial completed the end-of-life protocol.

CHAPTER 3

BLUE COCOON

Libby fell asleep before the end of the family saga was revealed. She remained quiet and still in her cocoon as her thoughts turned to Uncle Johnny and an uncle who she never knew existed.

The postmortem tidying up gave her time to plan the escape from her casket. After all, Libby couldn't leave her hiding place until both men had left the morgue.

She entertained herself by ruminating on the countless funerals she had witnessed. Libby had not necessarily been present at all of the morose happenings, but she was often mentally aware of the ethereal protocol involved in the journey of the dead through Blue Haven. Palm trees loomed, votive candles burned, and the sickeningly sweet smell of lilies permeated her life. Stiff, waxy gladioli reminded her of dead bodies frozen in eternity. Still, she dealt with all of this and kept it in perspective.

While the game of hiding in a display coffin was a source of morbid pleasure for her, playing with dolls was in fact a ruse. Libby had always been intrigued by the conversations of others, and she had a talent for sleuthing along with a great imagination. The ability to combine truth and fiction was hers to claim and was a source of many hours of self-indulgent fantasy. The security and safety of the cocoon of blue velvet allowed rampant thoughts and delicate manipulations of factual matters in her mind.

The familiar buzz of the intercom announced that the guys were being summoned by Emm for cocktails at six and dinner to follow.

Leo and Andy showered in the anteroom and changed into casual clothes. Emm did not allow the smell of formaldehyde in her house. It was lights out in the morgue and through the repose room to the elevator. They looked forward to a martini and prime rib dinner.

***

Libby flattened herself into the casket and held her breath as Leo and Andy passed by. The elevator door opened and closed. She savored the silence. This clandestine witness to conversation between her dad and the medical examiner would eventually play out in a family secret being solved. The familiar sound of the elevator as it lumbered its way up four levels told her that she had time to put her plan into action.

Andy asked, "By the way Leo, what does Libby think of all this malarkey about her uncles?"

"She knows only about visiting family in Texas. No need to confuse her about Earle just yet. I will explain it all at the airport before he shows up."

"Nothing like procrastination, Leo. Jesus H. Christ! You leave in a few days. Tell her now." Andy couldn't contain his concern.

"Not going to happen, Andy. I don't want to deal with her endless barrage of questions until the last possible minute!"

"Whatever you say, my friend!"

"By the way, Emm and I are very grateful to you for agreeing to step in here while I'm gone. I know you and Emm, along with the staff, can handle the shop. If all hell breaks loose, send clients to Madison to Digbee for the messy stuff and load 'em back here for viewing and hand-wringing. Can't thank you enough, old buddy!"

"Let's see how thankful you are when you get my bill, you old curmudgeon." Andy had a knack for turning sentimentality into reality.

***

Libby heard the ding of the elevator as it arrived at each of the four floors. She knew there was time to escape. She launched herself out of her tomb, and with one giant leap, she landed with a thud onto the floor. She ran toward the hidden staircase behind the blue velvet drapes and darted up the back stairs. She arrived in the hall just as the lift door opened.

Leo greeted her with a big hug and inquired about her day.

If only he knew! A moment of guilt washed over her, but her recovery was quick and complete. Her excitement about the trip was contained. It was best to act composed and not let on that a great surprise was in store.

CHAPTER 4

WAITING GAME BLUES

The three went into the parlor where Emm greeted them with refreshments before dinner.

Lib and Len slurped their cokes, and the adults sipped their martinis.

"Libby, go check out the surprise on the desk." Leo pointed to the envelope on the marble desktop.

She ran over, grabbed the manila envelope, and tore it open. The plane tickets to Del Rio were inside. "Wow, are we really going to Texas—just you and me—Dad? Can we leave tonight?" Libby never lacked enthusiasm when a new adventure was presented. She did cartwheels up and down the great hall with reckless abandon.

Len watched this with a great sadness that did not go unnoticed by Leo.

"Son, go and look out of the dining room window."

Len ran over and pushed the heavy blue drapes aside. There was a brand-new ten-speed bike on the lawn—the one that he had seen at the Western Auto in town. He ran past Libby's endless show of gymnastics and flew out the door and onto the bike. His legs were just long enough to reach the ground. He jumped onto the bike, wobbled his way down the driveway, and yelled, "This is way better than Texas. Yahoo!"

Another round of cocktails was called for to celebrate the happiness of children.

The family and friend gathered around the dining room table, which was set with Emm's beautiful china and Waterford crystal. Emm brought out the rib roast, creamed spinach, roasted potatoes, and Yorkshire pudding with gravy.

Leo poured the Merlot, and Andy carved the roast. Cutting meat was his forte.

***

That night in bed, Libby's mind wandered, and she fantasized about flying on a big jet and spending the long Thanksgiving holiday with her dad and his family. She slipped into slumber and dreamland without a care in her sixteen-year-old world.

Her alarm was set for five o'clock, and when it rang, Libby hit the ground running. So much to do and so little time. Tuesday was the departure day, so the next few days were the preparation for her vacation.

After breakfast, it was time to shop for gifts for the Texas members of the Carlow family. Emm's mantra was "Never arrive anywhere empty-handed." Books about lobster boats, T-shirts with Maine logos, and maple syrup were the goodies to be transported.

After all, it was good to start off on the right foot.

CHAPTER 5

BLUEBIRD FLIGHT

Once the passengers were loaded and the luggage was stashed into Emm's Volvo, the whole family was on its way to the Augusta airport.

"I'm afraid to ask if you and Libby have had that chat yet?" Emm's jaw tightened in anticipation of her husband's answer.

"Not yet," Leo replied.

Emm scowled at Leo. His inability to have a very important conversation with their daughter didn't surprise her.

Libby listened intently from the back seat.

Leo planned to tell Libby that his younger brother, Earle, would be joining them on the flight, but there was plenty of time to talk with her as they waited for the flight.

They reached the Augusta airport and parked curbside at the Northeast Yellowbird gate. This flight would connect to Boston, Atlanta, and ultimately San Antonio before a quick commuter flight to Del Rio.

Libby's curiosity had reached warp speed, and her nonstop chatter was a major distraction to the tasks at hand.

"We need to collect our baggage and kiss Mum and Len goodbye—and then I will explain a few things to you." Leo's voice told Libby that this would be an important reveal.

After goodbyes all around, Len and Emm drove off. Libby waved until the Volvo was out of sight.

The porter loaded their bags on his trolley, and Leo and Libby followed behind.

It was time for Leo to release the burden of the complicated family history of his father, Jack Carlow, to Libby. He cleared his throat and allowed all the bitterness and feelings of abandonment to start the bilious climb of suppressed emotion from his throat. Where to start was Leo's dilemma. "Another person will be joining us on our trip today. He is my younger brother, Earle."

Libby was taken aback, and questions swirled in her head. She waited to hear more.

Leo recounted that three sons were born to Jack and Vera Carlow. The family was not able to stay together after Vera's death. Jack had to work, and his only option was to leave the three boys with their mother's relatives. The brothers were separated and grew up miles apart in Maine. Leo was amazed at her reaction. Libby was quiet and still, which he had not expected.

As he continued with the family update, he saw a familiar figure approach. He knew immediately that it was Earle. The boyish grin and slight swaggering walk said it all.

The brothers embraced and clapped each other on the back the way guys do.

"Jumpin' gee hossafat, you look just like Dad," said Earle.

Leo was the oldest son, but to the younger brother, he was a father figure—even though only three years separated them.

"You look the same to me, little brother!" Leo held back his feelings of love as he had learned to do over the years.

"Meet your niece, Elizabeth Vera Carlow, or as she is known to us: Libby."

Libby held out her hand, but the next thing she knew, she was swept up in the air, spun around, and hugged to her uncle's chest.

The three stood in the terminal chattering all at once while years of separation melted away. After all, blood is thicker than water, isn't it?

CHAPTER 6

BOSTON AND BEYOND

The family checked in at the Augusta airport before they boarded their Boston flight. All the details were attended to efficiently. Luggage was weighed and tagged, tickets were stamped, boarding passes were issued, and the flight number was finally called.

The three of them stepped out into the November sunshine and followed the path to the aircraft and up the metal stairs and onto the DC-3, the pride of the Northeast Yellowbird fleet. The seats were big and plush, and the overhead bins were roomy. The ample legroom provided solid comfort. The passageway door was closed and secured, the carry-on bags were stowed, the seat belts were fastened, and the tray tables were put away. After the passengers were given briefings by the stewardesses, it was time to fly.

The engines roared, and the propellers vanished in rapid whirling motion as the plane taxied down the runway, faster and faster until the split second when the passengers and crew felt contact with earth fall away.

The flight passed quickly, and the Boston skyline was soon visible. The descent into Logan Airport was turbulent, owing to thunderstorms in the area. Warning lights flashed and advised passengers to remain seated and belted. The plane landed with skids and thuds, and it finally came to a halt with a violent jerk.

Leo, unable to resist his assessment of the landing, remarked to Earle, "Jesus, even I could have made a better landing—and I'm not even a pilot!"

"Leo, my wise brother, any landing that we walk away from is a good one!"

The departure from the plane and descent onto the tarmac were an adventure. Torrential rain and lightning strikes surrounded the terminal. Luggage on trolleys was being sorted and loaded onto waiting planes for the next leg of the journey. Once inside the terminal, the gate was clearly visible. There was no time to spare.

Enjoying the same good luck throughout the trip remained to be seen; correct bags going to correct destination, good food, easy flight, and no thunderstorms would be marvelous. With tickets stamped and flight time confirmed and on schedule, life would be simple.

"Flight 237 to Atlanta continuing onto San Antonio now boarding at gate three."

This was the awaited call to fly on the giant Boeing 727.

Passengers lined up and presented boarding passes before the long walk down the canopied passageway that connected terminal to plane. Everyone scurried, anxious to have first dibs on overhead bins and find their assigned seats.

Libby slid into the window seat and was followed by Leo and Earle.

Finally, they were on their way. The sound of the ramp being disengaged and hatch doors being slammed shut and secured reinforced the reality of the moment and the isolation from the outside world.

The passengers were briefed by the stewardesses, and they concluded their instructions with proper use of oxygen masks and the locations of exits and flotation devices.

The engines engaged and vibrated with such powerful force that all other sounds ceased. The smell of jet fuel, faint but distinctive, permeated the cabin. Chock blocks were removed from the massive tires with a great clunk, and the aircraft started a slow, deliberate motion toward the taxiway. The powerful engines propelled the great plane at a dizzying speed until the runway was left behind in a trail of smoke.

***

The sensation of flying was new to Libby, but as a fighter pilot in WWII, Uncle Earle had been assigned to the Fourth Fighter Group stationed in England. He had never spoken of his experiences, and even his brothers knew little of his wartime history. The virtue of keeping secrets had always served the Carlow family well in both war and in peace. Why change the program now? After all, it had been a way of life for many years on many different levels. No one had ever been harmed by living with illusion, lies, and deceit. As long as everyone was happy—and no harm was done—what difference did it make?

The pilot confirmed the destination and estimated arrival time. "Sunny skies, cruising altitude of thirty thousand feet, and local temperature of eighty degrees in Atlanta. Enjoy flying with Delta." The pilot clicked off the intercom.

Cocktail time was announced. After all, it was five o'clock somewhere.

Leo ordered a double gin martini, Libby asked for a coke, and Earle requested a double scotch on the rocks. Dinner would be served soon, which was one of the best perks of flying!

Dinner was being rolled out: roast pork, baked potato, string beans, and apple dumpling.

Nice! Cocktails and a meal were included in the ticket price. Belly full and after-dinner scotch consumed, Earle settled back in his seat and was finally able to relax.

The flight began to remind Earle of when he had been shot down over France in March 1944. He heard the sound of aircraft engines, he was surrounded by endless clouds, and he felt the pulsing of the aircraft as it burst through the blue sky. These sensations began to evoke past details of a time and place that he never wanted to visit again.

Thoughts became blurred, and dreams soon replaced those thoughts with memories.

CHAPTER 7

BLUE HORIZON

March 1944

I was back in England at my airfield in Debden. I slowly woke from deep, alcohol-induced sleep, and I thought about how I ended up here as a commissioned officer and pilot. It still seemed a dream or maybe a nightmare.

I left Maine and joined the Royal Canadian Air Force in 1941. This allowed me to go to pilot training and join in the war effort. There was a minor hitch: I had to give up my American citizenship to accomplish this. Lots of my buddies did the same thing since the United States had not yet joined the war.

Being trained as a pilot in Saskatchewan, Canada, guaranteed being shipped to England to fly for the Brits. I was shipped directly to Debden after one year of pilot training. When the United States entered the war in 1941, all of us Yanks who flew for the Canadians had our American citizenship reinstated. We were sucked up into the United States Army Air Corps, which eventually became the United States Air Force.

My hangover on that cold, foggy morning added to the burden I carried. The recent news of a pregnancy that resulted from a liaison with a married British woman reminded me of the danger of thinking with the "little head." The first night I saw her at the Chez Moi club, I was in love.

As the Brits said, "You Yanks are oversexed, overpaid, overfed, and over here."

They were right. Some called the Chez Moi by its nickname, The Canadian Riding Club, for reasons that should not be explained.

She and I had a platonic relationship for many months. Thanks to her, I got to know many British people and visited many places. She was an ambulance driver in the Civil Defense Service in London. She and I, along with her friends Marg and Kath and their mates, were inseparable.

We all went on holiday to River Lee, a small village near a river of the same name. I had a weak moment and have regretted the intimacy ever since. She was married to a British soldier, and I was engaged to my high school sweetheart back home. *What was I thinking?* I slammed down hot tea to clear my head. *What's wrong with a bloody country that drinks tea instead of coffee for a hangover? No wonder they are losing the war!*

I headed over to the Quonset hut for the day's briefing.

At zero dark thirty, the room quickly filled up with air crews eager to learn about the day's mission. I took a seat alongside my fellow officers and fell into the urgency of the moment. We would be briefed today by Colonel Fuller, also known as "the long bony finger" because if he pointed at you, it would not be good!

Today's rodeo would be for twenty P-51 fighter planes, aka Mustangs, to fly cover for eighty B-17 bombers, launching out of Lavenham Airfield in Britain and heading to Berlin. After we ditched the bombers in Germany, we would be engaged in strafing runs over France on the way back home to Debden. This would be a five-hour flight over many concentrations of flak. We discussed rendezvous points and times, received weather updates, and hacked our watches, completing the briefing.

We would be dispersed into five groups of four. Each P-51 would fly protective cover for about four B-17s. The giant bombers were sitting ducks for the enemy since their great lumbering size restricted their ability to evade bullets.

It was time to earn our pay. We hustled off to the locker room and readied ourselves to fly and fight.

We pulled on flight suits and buckled the Mae West life vests in place. Next came fur-lined boots, leather helmets, and pouches filled with gold coins, which were essential if we were shot down and had to deal with the French Underground.

I secured my nine-millimeter Beretta in a holster under my armpit. I always kept it loaded with safety on. It made no sense to load a gun while looking down the barrel of an enemy rifle. I added goggles, fur-lined gloves, and silk topographical maps, which were tucked into my boots. To be alone over enemy territory would be bad enough, but without these essentials, there would be little chance of survival at any level. I felt a momentary chill, and then I shook it off. No worries! I headed out to airfield, climbed aboard my plane, and strapped on my parachute.

I was the lead pilot of the four Mustangs in my flight today, and I felt the full responsibility for the success of the mission, which included the safe return of the crew back to base. Three of us were old heads at the game, but one new guy was a little squirrely. He needed some reassurance. We all gave him the thumbs-up as we walked by. A cavalier attitude helped abate fear without seeming too maudlin.

The preflight check of my plane consisted of tire kicks and securing the connection of the two drop tanks. This extra fuel might save my ass if I ran low over the English Channel on my way home. I climbed the ladder to the cockpit and started the trusty Merlin engine. A few pops and bangs, a big roar, and a burst of black smoke kicked life into my little friend. The gauges all worked, and instrument checks were ongoing throughout the flight.

I taxied out and onto the green turf runway and closed the canopy. The other three P-51s fell in behind one by one. We each, in turn, held up our right thumbs. We kept the ends cut off of each leather glove because it was the only way to determine if we were sufficiently oxygenated in order to avoid hypoxia in flight. A blue thumb meant we had to drop to a lower altitude and allow our bodies to recover from the lack of oxygen. Our masks provided us with pure oxygen, but they were ill fitting and cumbersome. It was common for masks to loosen in a dogfight, which could cause hypoxia, confusion, or death.

The orange-and-white checkered flag was waved in a circle and dropped. It was the signal for me to advance with my flight first and for the other sixteen Mustangs to follow in groups of four.

We left the turf in formation, but we would break away in flight at timed intervals to keep prop wash at a minimum for the guys behind us.

Up and over the trees and into the blue sky at five thousand feet. Home again! Our flight path over familiar scenery didn't last long. We climbed quickly to twenty thousand feet and soared in and out of clouds—all of us warriors in sight of each other.

I went over the morning's briefing in my mind. Our mission, consisting of twenty P-51s, was to cozy up to eighty B-17 bombers on their way to bomb Berlin. The bombers, assigned to the Eighth Air Force, would launch first from their base. We launched, and once airborne, the lead crews would work out the details with each other. It was a big production. *The Third Reich is in for trouble!*

I reminisced about the forty-plus missions that we had flown over Europe. I thought about how the Fourth Fighter Group, my unit, had provided hours of protection for these bombers. These giants of the air were civilization's only hope as Eisenhower saw it. Bombing the infrastructure of enemy country was the only way to quell the demonic obsession of Adolf Hitler.

Decimation of the Third Reich is the key to ending this terrible war. Our mission is to destroy railroads, trains, roads, farms, and troops—no matter what collateral damage ensues! This war shit is tough business! It is said, "Old men declare war, and young men fight!" Enough ruminating. It's time to do my job and time to lock and load!

We flew in and around clouds, and over the Dover Cliffs and the English Channel. Off in the distance, the B-17s came into view. The bombers looked like looming, dark thunderstorms on the horizon. Bad weather ahead for Germany!

We rounded up with the bombers and began jockeying around them as we surveyed the situation.

My flight of Mustangs was now flying about two thousand feet above the B-17s that were at about twenty thousand feet. Each flight of four Mustangs began cutting the behemoths out of their pack like cowboys wrangling cows out of the herd. Theoretically, four P-51s would provide adequate cover for twenty B-17s, and so on, until all eighty planes felt safer in our presence.

I was on a hot microphone with their lead pilot, Colonel Ripley Russell. The "Ripper" and I discussed target areas and our breakaway plan in code.

France was now dead ahead, and the North Sea was portside. We crossed the southern tip of Belgium, over Luxembourg, and into Germany.

The bombers' targets waited beyond the Elbe River. Train tracks and munition dumps were visible to all in flight. After a few more minutes, we would bid adieu to our traveling companions.

We broke away from the B-17s and left the big boys on their own. After they had bombed everything in sight, they would find their way back from the target area to a fighter escort range. At that point, a rear cover wing of another fighter group would pick them up and drag them back to their home base.

The first leg of our mission was completed without any mishaps, and we headed back to France to finish the job laid out in the morning briefing. On the way, we headed to Paris and knocked out a few train tracks.

I dropped down to two hundred feet above the ground and announced, "Don't fire 'til you see the whites of their eyes!" It was not an original thought, but perspective was gained in the narrative.

The train tracks were sitting ducks. The strafing runs lasted about five minutes. We continued to pound the targets with twenty-millimeter machine guns mounted in the wings as we circled counterclockwise and targeted the area again. Ground fire was being returned. It was time to get out and move to the next target in the vicinity of Bergerac.

Three planes veered out from behind me and to the south of our position. Somewhere near Paris, we started our strafing maneuver again. We wreaked havoc on clusters of German tanks that appeared to be waiting to advance toward the French coastline.

My P-51s followed the Dordogne River toward the English Channel and home. *Not done yet!* Suddenly, out of nowhere, came a lone Messerschmitt looking for a fight. The group dispersed and returned fire. *Every man for himself!* Planes and bullets flew everywhere. We divided and attacked the German plane in random patterns. He ultimately ended up in a nine o'clock position, and the four of us were on the opposite side of the clock. *Boom! He's toast!*

Just as we reveled in victory, ground fire exploded around us. Just east of Angouleme, my plane shook with terrible violence. A twenty-millimeter shell had hit my fuselage, and flames poured into the cockpit on the starboard side. *No choice but to bail out.* I remembered the last words from the officer at our briefing this morning: "Never bail out over the area that you have just shelled." *Seems like timely advice—too bad I can't follow it!*

I quickly climbed to fifteen hundred feet, jettisoned the canopy, and pulled the stick back. My little plane dropped out from under me. My chute launched me up into a sea of black smoke.

Christ—now what? I pulled the rip cord, and my chute opened and twisted me like a pretzel. The wind was blowing a gale, but I was able to untangle my chute lines. The trick would be landing with all body parts intact.

I landed one hundred yards from my burning plane and walked away unscathed. March 1, 1944, will live in my memory forever!

CHAPTER 8

BLUE HEAVEN

March 1944

I quickly gathered up my chute and gear and hid in a raspberry patch. Voices surrounded me and were getting closer. I dropped my gear and ran for my life! People poured out of a small village and ran toward me. Bogged down in thick underbrush, I was unable to run with vines tangled around my legs and feet. I still hadn't been seen, so I crawled toward a grove of birch trees.

A Frenchman cutting wood nearby looked up at me and nodded.

I whispered as loud as I dared, "*Je suis* American!"

No response from him, but I approached anyway. He motioned me into the woods behind him and then followed me. I removed my leather jacket and held it out to him.

I pulled at his woolen overcoat and said, "*Changez vos vetements, avec moi?*" I was wearing a battle tunic and stood out like a sore thumb! His coat would allow me to blend in with the locals.

He unbuttoned his coat, handed it to me with a big, toothless grin, and said, "*Oui, oui maintenant, allez vous en vite vite!*"

I followed his command and ran to a nearby stand of trees.

My high school French teacher saved my ass today! God bless Madam Quirion! I will look her up when I get back to Maine—if I ever get back. Friggin' Nazis everywhere!

The leather jacket looked good on the Frenchman. I, on the other hand, looked rather peasantlike in the baggy coat.

He stood next to my tree and watched as I pulled my silk map out of my boot. He pointed to my position as near Angouleme, northwest of Nontron and Thiviers. Spain was southwest of me, and that was my goal. Any direction other than south would be suicide.

Spain was technically a neutral country at this point since Dictator Franco, a Nationalist, had not yet aligned with the Allies or the Germans.

We heard a commotion near the woods. The Frenchman motioned for me to hit the dirt and wait. He walked to the edge of the woods to investigate the noise. A few minutes later, he yelled to me, "Vite vite!" He motioned for me to run.

I trusted him. I ran to the opposite side of the trees, but there were no hiding places to be found! I burrowed under a fallen log and watched as a small jeep passed by with four German officers on board. They traveled at a fast clip, and the dust that billowed all around hid me in my vulnerable spot. The jeep disappeared around the corner, and I breathed a sigh of relief.

Farmers who were working in open fields seemed to not notice me, but I was not ready to be seen yet, not knowing if I trusted them.

Off in the distance, a wagon approached from the west. I was surely being watched, but who were the watchers? I stepped out of the woods into ruts made by wagon tracks and slowed my pace deliberately. The cart slowed as well, and the people in the cart motioned for me to walk ahead of them. We looked like a family returning from market as we traveled toward the outskirts of another village.

I couldn't help looking back over my shoulder at these brave and wonderful people who had helped me. They must have heard about a downed American plane in the area and a pilot who survived. They returned my glances with nods of approval. Clearly, they knew that the Yanks were risking their lives to give them liberty. I guess they were returning the favor.

I stopped at the edge of the village, even though they urged me to continue with them, because I was afraid. With my meager French and their marginal English, we managed to understand each other. I jumped into the cart, and they covered me with a rug. We drove to a train station in the village of Nontron. They told me to go there and wait for the next train to Thiviers, which would be along soon.

A young woman hopped out of the cart and returned with train tickets for me. I slipped a gold coin into her hand, but she refused the money. I discretely dropped the coin into her pocket.

The family handed me a bag of fruit, bread, and chocolate to sustain me until my next friendly encounter, whenever that might be. They knew that traveling with them was a risk for all of us since the Germans continually checked their homes and barns for escapees. I jumped out of the cart and rolled into a ditch. I knew that waiting for this train today would be too dangerous. I was on my own.

I headed to the perimeter of the town. I knew that I would not be on the train to Nontron today, and I decided to travel toward the setting sun, in a westward direction.

A farmer working horses in a field waved at me with both arms.

As I approached, I saw a family pitching hay onto a cart. They pointed to a wagon and told me, with sign language, to slide underneath and wait.

The farmer used his limited command of English and confided that they were too afraid to shelter me in their home, but his wife had gone to fetch an English woman who could help me with directions and news of enemies in the area.

The English lady owned a pastry shop in the nearby village and was privy to much gossip that concerned the occupation. It seemed the Nazis liked coffee and pastries as they exchanged secret information with each other. They had no idea that the pastry chef spoke German.

She told me to avoid the village at all costs. The Germans knew of an American pilot who had walked away from a plane crash, and they had been searching for him with dogs.

Priceless information!

She handed me a bag of pastries, wine, and fruit and wished me well.

I pressed on down a dirt road and retraced my steps. Reality had set in, and I needed help. I had a plan to make it to Spain, but accomplishing it on my own seemed a daunting task.

As I continued walking and feeling sorry for myself, a large farmhouse appeared on the horizon. I headed in that direction and thought help might be found here. *But what if I find Germans there?* At any rate, I had already been seen by people on the front porch.

Bloody hell! I need water. I will take a chance. I said, *"Avez vous l'eau pour moi?"*

"Oui," they responded quickly.

At that moment, a group of Frenchmen in berets and baggy clothes came out of the house. A jug of water was handed to me, and one of them asked me, in English, if I wanted to go to Paris. I replied that Spain was my destination because I knew that Paris was crawling with Germans. I needed to head south toward the Pyrenees and the neutrality of Spain in order to have any chance of returning to Britain.

My new acquaintances suddenly engaged in a heated exchange among themselves, and they finally decided that I was right. With that, I was taken into their home and provided with a hot bath, clean clothes, and a room with a feather bed. Little did I know that the reveal at the supper table would fill me with great joy!

I had found my way into the much-revered French Underground!

CHAPTER 9

BLUE CHALLENGE

The aroma of coffee brewing brought me out of a deep sleep. I had no idea of time since my watch had been destroyed in my bailout. I dressed quickly, crawled down my loft ladder, and received a round of applause and a mock salute from the characters at the table.

"You must be an important general, *mon ami*, to be such a late sleeper. It is seven o'clock here in the real world!" scoffed one of the Frenchmen.

"As the Brits would say, are you taking the mickey out of me?" I replied.

"Oui, oui!" they replied.

I thought they didn't a clue about British humor, but just as well since I couldn't possibly explain what *mickey* was anyway.

Breakfast was a feast crowned by mugs of coffee with dollops of rich cream that clung to my mustache with every slurp. The meal was finished, and the table was covered with a map of southern France, the western Pyrenees, and Spain. Many cities and open areas had been marked with an X to denote avoidance for escapees. My new comrades continued to argue in French, and they pounded their fists into the table, presumably to try to convince each other of the best route to follow. I listened intently, and then I pulled out my trusty silk map from my boot. I proceeded to show them what I believed was a good start to a plan. I shared my thoughts and encouraged they could make corrections.

My plan was to travel eastward from our location here in Angouleme and then on to Nontron and Thiviers. My silk map had clearly defined roads and villages and was more current than theirs.

They argued incessantly and decided to add another voice to the fray. Two of them left and returned with Jean Pierre, who would be my guide.

Jean Pierre jumped in to the discussion and said, "So, this is our Yankee pilot, eh? Welcome to France, mon ami. Even though you hadn't planned a visit here, you are in the hands of the best travel agents in the world!"

I liked the guy. He seemed like a rational man who spoke superb English. We checked my map against theirs, and he decided my map was better. Jean Pierre would be my guide in the beginning, but things might be subject to change. We evaluated my initial plan, but he had a better plan in mind. We created a solid plan that we hoped would stand up to impromptu changes along the way.

He liked the first part of my plan and then added his plan to mine. We would eventually work our way westward through Perigueux, Bergerac, Marmande, and Oloron Sainte Marie, near Spain. There, he would turn me over to a new guide who would take me over the Pyrenees since mountain climbing was not his expertise. Jean explained that only the best mountaineers in the Underground would attempt this trip over the Pyrenees.

I whispered softly to myself, "Great! Where do I sign up?"

"Did you say something?" Jean asked.

"No," I replied.

He continued on and said that we might pick up more "souls" throughout the journey. He briefed me with this unbelievably detailed plan. Pamplona would be the drop-off point. From there—since commercial flights out of Pamplona were nonexistent—I would travel by bus or train to Gibraltar. From there, hopefully, I would hop either a British merchant ship or a flight to the UK.

Sounds easy.

Jean said, "The details, like train and bus tickets, will be provided for us through the Underground—since we work with the locals—and Catholic churches along the way. We have no shortage of religion in this country—lucky for us."

He amazed me with his knowledge and resolve to keep me safe.

Jean said, "Tomorrow, we pick up new identity papers for you. Prepare to be a deaf-mute traveling with me to visit family. You must play this game while we travel because there may be many watchers and listeners out there who will turn us both over to the Nazis in a minute. It would be quite a coup for them to get their hands on an American pilot and, at the same time, a member of the French Resistance. We must not let this happen. We will use our weapons on ourselves if necessary to avoid capture!"

I pressed my arm firmly against my armpit. The handle of the pistol nestled in place eased my mind. Evening was upon us, and after a fine meal was finished, we drank and listened to music for entertainment. *Time to hit the sack and suffer fitful sleep.*

***

I woke before the rooster crowed.

We gathered all the provisions that we could carry. We stuffed boiled eggs, parsnips, bread, cheese, raw potatoes, and wine into grain bags that would serve as bedding on our journey. Water would be readily available along the route. We loaded up coins, compasses, matches, twine, knives, and sidearms and followed the train tracks to Nontron, still wary of our surroundings and avoiding the creation of any suspicion.

After a short trek, we found the train station and bought tickets that would take us from Nontron to Thiviers. We were planning to take the train from Thiviers to Perigueux, but we realized that we would arrive after the eleven o'clock curfew. That was not a good plan because the curfew times were strictly enforced by the Germans. We needed to rethink our operational tactics. During the day, we could blend in with the locals, but after dark, we would be targets for questioning by the Gestapo. Many able-bodied citizens were rounded up for potential labor camp recruitment, including boys, girls, and women who filled other useful purposes for the Third Reich.

We decided to avoid Thiviers altogether. Instead, we bought tickets out of Nontron to Limoges. Even though Limoges was northeast of our planned travel route and might add days to the overall journey, we felt it was a better option than vacationing in Germany. We now would be avoiding a German stronghold and would continue south to Spain with no detection.

We arrived in Limoges just before dark. Jean Pierre was contacted by our group and informed of increased Gestapo activity in town. *Shit! Out of the frying pan and into the fire!*

We were told to lay low, but curfew was approaching. We took a chance and went directly to the hotel near the train station in hopes that the soldiers would be in party mode and not looking for wanderers to harass. We stashed our gear behind an old shed near an abandoned shack and proceeded to the hotel.

We turned the collars of our peasant coats up to hide our faces and entered the quiet building. No one was around.

Jean approached the hotel clerk behind the desk. As Jean registered us, I stood behind him. My ears were stuffed with cotton wool to help with my pretense of being deaf. He passed our identification cards to the clerk to confirm our French citizenry. My card also confirmed that I was deaf and dumb. *Good cover! These Frenchmen had thought of everything.*

The staircase that led to our room was guarded by two German sentries. We kept our eyes on the floor and went unnoticed as we quickly climbed the stairs. We settled into our room and opened a bottle of wine smuggled inside my coat pocket. A parsnip assuaged our hunger. We fell on the beds exhausted.

A loud pounding on the door brought us to our feet.

For Christ's sake. Now what?

Jean opened the door slowly, expecting to see the sentries, and I drew my pistol from under my pillow and prepared to kiss my ass goodbye. I would at least go down in a hail of bullets.

False alarm.

The desk clerk needed our ages on the registry.

We went back to bed, but we both slept with one foot on the floor.

CHAPTER 10

BLUE HAZE

We woke to greet the fourth day of our journey and planned to catch the early train to Perigueux. We got off before the last stop, disappeared into the countryside, and hid in the woods. We walked about five kilometers before we stopped near a small stream and drank our fill of fresh water. We bathed for the first time in days. *What a treat!* We filled up on parsnips, stale bread, and cheese. *Feast!* Sleep called us, and we slept on moss-covered ground under fir trees.

The next morning, we deduced that were south of Perigueux. The coming week or so should put us just beyond Bergerac, where we would meet with a contact person near Marmande. Since we were ahead of schedule, we stayed safely in the woods all day and through the night.

The flora and fauna that surrounded us imparted a sense of a "bit of all right," as the Brits said. I realized that I missed the "Brit chat," which can't be described in any other language.

The days blurred together, and trains, buses, wagons, and horses all looked the same. There was no sign of the German invasion as we headed toward Marmande. We were still many miles from Paris.

We were scheduled to meet with our liaisons near a stable on the edge of Marmande. Jean Pierre decided to go alone to the appointed meeting spot since he was familiar with the area. He returned much later without having met our guy. We made camp in the woods that night and hoped to have better luck the next day.

The next morning, we went together and had a successful meeting with our contacts. We were resupplied with food and told to continue traveling on local trains. They handed us tickets to Oloron. There would be many small villages between here and our trail to freedom, but Oloron would be our last village serviced by rail in France. The plan was to meet our next contact there, and he would hook us up with our alpine guide who would take us across the Pyrenees and on to Pamplona. We boarded the train and looked forward—with trepidation—to our next adventure.

Our train stopped in a small village outside of our destination. We thought it might be too soon to leave the train, but all the landmarks that we had been told to look for were right in front of our eyes: a red farmhouse, a corral with workhorses, and dense woods. That would be the place where we would make contact with Underground personnel.

Jean and I ambled off into the woods and made a small campsite that was not visible from the road. Night was approaching, and we ate cold food and bedded down.

***

In the morning, Jean went into the village center to find the location of the Catholic church connected with the Underground. After a three-hour wait, Jean returned to our camp alone. We played this game for a few more days without any sign of our liaison.

On the third day, we entered the church together and knelt in a pew. Jean was a good Catholic and a convincing parishioner. I was just along for the ride. We continued this pattern of humbling behavior for two days. The villagers must have thought we had much to pray about or confess. We were praying all right—for someone to tell us what to do next!

On the afternoon of the fifth day, as we knelt in the church, we heard the tinkling of a bell behind the sacristy. A priest motioned for us to follow him.

Is this our guy?

We walked down a long hall, down a long staircase, and into a large room that housed religious artifacts, brass candlesticks, and collectibles. Wooden wine racks that were built into the wall at the far end of the room held many bottles of wine from different vintners. *We might have a wine connoisseur on our hands.*

Just as we wondered what was in store for us, the priest nodded at us and said, "I am Father Lee. Welcome to the house of God and his branch of the French Resistance movement. You are safe here."

Needless to say, we both breathed a sigh of relief. We knew that we could trust Father Lee.

He proceeded toward the wine collection, removed a few bottles, and released a lever that was cleverly concealed behind the Merlot. A small door swung open to reveal a narrow entrance to another room. He motioned for us to enter. It was a large, comfortable room with bunk beds, a sofa, cozy chairs, and a small piano in the corner. In the center was a long table with chairs all around it. We were informed that this would be home for a while—until safe travel could be ensured.

Our priest went on to tell us that the original contact person who was to have met us there had been exposed as a German spy who had infiltrated the Underground. Upon this revelation, he was shot. The Resistance forces took no prisoners.

Father Lee added, "We don't take kindly to traitors. Now go, gather your belongings, and relax here for a bit."

We obliged, returned to the church with our gear, and settled into our cozy wine cellar.

Father Lee shared with us that many souls had used this room while awaiting safe passage through the next leg of their journey.

That evening, we enjoyed a wonderful meal prepared by Father Lee's housekeeper. He referred to her as "precious Edith," and her gentle demeanor and welcoming manner made us feel special indeed. The loving glances exchanged between the two hinted at a more familiar relationship than man of the cloth and housekeeper.

The four of us sat together at the table and shared wine and stories.

Apparently, Edith was well-known in the region as a gourmet cook. Her lamb cassoulet, roasted vegetables, bread, and exquisite strawberry jam filled our empty bellies. After our meal, our charming hostess played piano and soothed our weary souls with song and music.

Father Lee had been instructed to tell us to wait here until our next guide contacted us. We were happy to spend a few more days with these delightful people and enjoy sharing their food and wine.

Jean and I met our next guide at our priest's dinner table in our private sanctuary on the third evening of our seclusion. We were introduced to Rene over our evening meal. He shared the story of his career in the French Foreign Legion. After the Germans surrendered in Algiers, he came back to France, his birthplace, and continued the fight with his countrymen.

As we stood up from the dinner table, I noticed that this six-foot man towered above us. His hands were the size of dinner plates, and his handshake left no doubt about who was in charge. He announced that Jean would not be traveling on with us. He had another role to fill in the absence of the German spy. Jean would have a new assignment.

As luck would have it, two traveling companions would be added to our group. They were fleeing France for Britain as well.

I was not very confident knowing my lifeline, Jean, would be leaving me. I began to wonder what kind of half-assed operation was being run there. As I looked querulously from priest to Jean and back to Rene, Father Lee assured me that the same plan would be followed, and we would still arrive at our destination in Pamplona in a timely manner. He told us the plan laid out by the French Resistance group was still in place.

Rene picked up the lead and explained that the choice route for us, given our location near Basque Country, was called the Comet Line, a walking path that would channel us through villages, farmland, and a number of reliable safe houses. The route was isolated, but it was longer and had more hazardous trails than the Pat Line, the other established route in the more eastern parts of France and Spain. Rene had information that General Franco's *Guardia Civil*, his Nationalist army, was more active in the Pat Line area. We would follow the route originally laid out near the Basque region.

Rene turned to me and asked, "Mon ami, are you happy to follow my directions and have me as your traveling companion on this journey?"

I answered, "Oui oui!" *Like I would argue with this guy! Maybe I should have stayed with my burning plane and roasted marshmallows!*

CHAPTER 11

BLUE MOON

The next morning, Rene and I boarded the train to Aire. This journey was like any other that we had taken, and I still play the part of a deaf-mute. We anxiously scanned the seats for any suspicious-looking characters who might be our traveling companions.

Rene and I settled into our humble seating area with farmers and peasants who were traveling to market with their wares. The smells of ripened goat cheese, bread, and bouquets of freshly cut lavender seemed like perfume of the gods. The smells filled the passenger car with the wonderful aroma of normal life in the French countryside.

As the people around us visited and chatted, a beautiful young woman in a blue smock and a black beret adjusted her long black hair and tied it in a bun. She sat very close to us—almost too close. She pulled out a skein of yarn from a tote bag and knitted furiously.

I thought, *Too corny to be real. Madam Defarge on a French train in the middle of nowhere in 1944? Blimey!* She clearly had the attention of Rene. He was fixated but cool, calm, and collected. *This is the contact.* A few seats over, a rumpled, unshaven, skinny man blended in with the locals and seemed to be somewhat simpleminded.

Rene whispered, "These are our people—but making ourselves known to them without creating suspicion may be a challenge."

The woman put down her knitting and fumbled for a cigarette case in her bag. She brought out tobacco and thin tissue paper and began to roll her own smoke.

Rene, master of control that he was, waited until the right moment. He leaned toward her with a match, struck the head with his thumbnail, and produced flame. Their eyes met, and at that moment, words did not matter.

The simple man observed all of this, flapped his arms inside the sleeves of his rumpled coat, as though acting the fool at having witnessed a semi-sexual encounter. *These are our people?*

The four of us were one; it was time to continue the game. They were the pros, and I was the newly initiated member. Even though I knew nothing about these two, the Resistance people had briefed them about me. Being a Yank who was shot down while strafing German munitions to save their asses apparently made me a hero. *Is it their love of France or the love of the gold coins they know I'm carrying that makes me special?* I had to believe that these people of the French Underground were not driven by gold coins alone. They believed in the fight for their independence from German invasion and that Allied forces were the only hope they had for achieving that goal. However, the compensation of gold to the people of the Resistance enabled them to sustain their personal existence while helping unfortunate bastards like me survive and tell our stories.

As we traveled along the countryside, I saw Rene's mind working hard to keep these new travelers close to us as per his instructions from his superiors. It seemed like body language and furtive glances were the only communication among the three of them. I was just along for the ride.

In addition to these two pickups, we would be connected with a boatman who would be transporting us across the Gave de Pau River. There, our alpine guide—the most critical member of our team—would join us for the trek across the Pyrenees. This person would have experience in all things related to mountaineering and elusive travel. Our guide would also be responsible for our safety, securing food sources, and creating a cohesive group of misfits with one unifying goal: freedom.

As the train lurched through the countryside, the view of vast nothingness changed to reveal a more populated area of villages and farmhouses meshed together. The landscape flattened and merged into gentle, sloping hills with scruffy underbrush. This began the upland terrain before the Pyrenees Mountains. All I saw were the bluffs of higher elevation that rose up in the mist. The train slowed down, and I saw a sign for Aire ahead. That part of the journey made my heart pound because the familiar was about to change. We left the train unnoticed, slipped away from the main road, and found safe refuge from the fast-approaching night.

Rene and I lagged behind our traveling companions, but it was understood that we would meet up before dark.

The landscape was more beautifully lush than I had expected. Palm trees, tall arborvitae, and hedges of pink, red, and purple flowers lined walkways and roads.

Rene spied a good source of camouflage behind some tall juniper bushes that were well away from the village and farms. We dawdled along and hoped for a sign from our buddies. We heard branches snap and muffled voices speaking French. We froze and held our breath! Quietly, the ragged man and the woman appeared off to the side. We were together again!

As darkness approached, we walked two by two, and we felt safe in our environment.

Our new companion was Elise, a British Army nurse, who had been assigned to a hospital in Paris. She chatted with us as though we were old friends, and she hung onto Rene with her body in close contact with his every step.

My walking buddy was Armand, a member of the Resistance. He was traveling to Pamplona, which happened to also be my destination. He didn't share his reasons for leaving his country, but it was easy enough to guess that he had been discovered as an enemy of the Nazis.

We were one in total darkness, save for a bright light in a small window ahead. Soon, there were many small lights and campfires that encircled wooden caravans.

Romany gypsies to be sure!

Rene scouted ahead, and we stayed behind—in plain sight of the campers.

These nomads were certainly headed for Spain. Given the history of the times, we surely would be welcomed into their camp since they knew we had gold: the currency of war. Rene returned and flashed a thumbs-up sign. He warned that we were invited to share food, but we were to follow his lead: no wine, no women, no dancing, and no palm readings!

We would eat, pay in gold, and leave. Rene reminded me to take the gold francs out of my money belt now, so that they could not see the amount I carried. Gypsies expected to be offered some form of payment in return for their hospitality. Since these nomads were known to be charming and then slit your throat, we must be on guard. We all nodded in agreement. My friends were more sophisticated than I was about the world of gypsies.

The aroma that came from giant iron caldrons placed over wood fires was wonderful. We sat around the fire and were given wooden bowls of stewed meat and vegetables roasted in rich gravy and spices. Giant slices of bread spread with soft, pungent cheese were plentiful. Bladders of wine were passed from one to another, but we abstained from drinking. I think they knew their reputation for lacing high-alcohol wine with hallucinogenic herbs preceded them. They laughed whenever we refused the drink.

All too soon, it was time to leave. I held out five francs to the woman who seemed to be in charge of the group. As she took the coin, I was momentarily dazzled by her gold teeth. I unwittingly allowed her to look at my empty palm. A loud wail came from her, unlike I had ever heard before. Her dark eyes filled with tears as she said to me in a broken French-Romany dialect, "*Tu mort sur l'aeroplane,* mon ami!"

I was taken aback by her words of *death* and *airplane*. I looked at Rene.

He laughed and said, "She thinks you will die in a plane crash, friggin' gypsy! Doesn't she know you already did that? Let's get out of here!"

We left the camp with ample supplies of bread and cheese—Romany gypsies are generous when motivated by gold francs—but we left the wine!

CHAPTER 12

BLUE DAWN

April 1944

We left the gypsy camp, and the four of us went out into the darkness. The smell of campfire smoke, pine needles, and damp moss made us want for creature comforts of warmth and rest. The moon was bright and guided us along a well-trodden path.

In the distance, Rene saw a recess in the hillside that looked like a cave. He went ahead and scouted the area. We followed with lit torches. Others had preceded us with the same thought of protection from the elements and seclusion. We nestled into pine boughs that were thoughtfully placed to insulate us from the cold floor. A few crude stools and makeshift tables indicated others had used this campsite before.

As the last nubs of our candles burned down with smoky light, Rene announced that he would stand first watch outside the cave. Armand and I were too tired to argue, and we let him have first watch. Armand would take the second watch, and I would take the last watch before dawn.

As sleep was overtaking me, I noticed Elise had left her nest and had gone to the entrance of the cave. *Maybe a last call of nature before sleep?* Time was elusive, and I woke with a start to see Armand had left his pine bed too. *Maybe his turn at watch?*

I tossed and turned only to be distracted by heavy breathing outside the cave. I crawled slowly toward the cave entrance to see Elise and Armand entwined in the last throes of the most intimate exchange between lovers. I retreated hastily back to my bed, embarrassed by my intrusion into their moment.

Sleep overtook my mind and body, but I woke with a start at first light. I scrambled outside, but I saw no one about. All the beds inside the cave were empty, and Rene and Armand were bathing in stream.

I said, "Where's Elise?"

They both looked at me and pointed to a fresh mound of earth a few hundred feet away. Vultures sat menacingly in nearby treetops.

I looked around in disbelief at the scene.

Rene scratched his head and said, "Armand and I knew from the beginning that part of this mission was to dispatch Elise. As a member of the Resistance, she used her position as head nurse in an Allied hospital in Paris to gather top-secret information from the Allies and pass it on to her high-ranking German lover. However, when Resistance people caught on to her game, they fed her erroneous information and used her as a decoy. She was told that she was valuable and was to continue her work in Spain. Little did she know she had just a few days to live—and crossing the Pyrenees with us was a ruse."

Armand said, "I know you must feel betrayed and sad at the same time, mon ami, but there is now one less double agent working both sides of the war. She never suspected that we were grooming her for the kill. When she saw the flash of my knife at her throat, her eyes told me everything I needed to know. She thought she was smarter than the rest of us, but the problem was that we weren't necessarily smarter—we just played harder to win!"

I felt gobsmacked! I speculated for a few moments and wondered what had caused her to make those deceitful decisions that ultimately took her life. *If only she had taken a different path. Perhaps her beauty and brains gave her a false sense of control and superiority over men. Too bad she took herself so seriously. In the end, she lost her life. Whatever the case, Elise was a brief but beautiful distraction for a country boy like me from Skowhegan, Maine.*

CHAPTER 13

WAY TO PAU

We trudged along quietly, and I thought of the many sacrifices that war brings. Our survival hinged not only on our ability to defend ourselves but on having each other's backs. My admiration for these brave Frenchmen was immeasurable. Their confidence and self-control would forever be a standard for the way I would live my life—if I would continue to have a life.

As I contemplated this deep thought, Rene opened his big trench coat, and thrust his hand into the deep pocket inside. "Mon ami, catch this!"

I looked up and caught what I thought was a baseball, but it turned out to be a hand grenade. Luckily, the pin was locked in place, but I still broke out in a sweat. "You could have given me a heads-up before lobbing this weapon at me!" I hollered. It was the first time I had ever seen a grenade up close and personal.

In his offhand manner, Rene replied, "Remember that when the pin is pulled, Mr. Grenade is not your friend!"

"Piss off, you crazy bastard!" I replied.

Rene said, "If you're going to play with us big boys, you had better be armed with our toys, eh?"

The walking was easy, and low shrubs and grassy fields surrounded us. Darkness was setting in as we follow the Louts River southwest toward Pau. We made camp at the opening of a cave on the riverbank and built a small fire to boil water for tea. *What a treat for a hot drink along with our meager rations. Tomorrow, we will be in Pau and be joined by Resistance people who will brief us on the latest movements of the enemy.*

As we relaxed by the fire, we opened the last bottle of Merlot to help ease our tired, aching feet. As we shared the wine, Armand felt like sharing his story with us. He told us how he was able to glean information from German officers while he worked as a bartender in Paris. He gained their trust by introducing them to French merchants who dealt in black market goods. One of these entrepreneurs was Coco Chanel, whose number 5 perfume was a highly desired commodity. Her desire to please the German army later came under scrutiny by the Allies.

Armand's ruse as a bartender lasted many months—until he was followed to the home of a known member of the Resistance. He was quickly removed from the streets, given a new identity, and then moved gradually out of circulation as a spy. When Elise surfaced as a collaborator, known only to the Underground, she was told that Armand would take her into Spain. She never knew that she had been found out by the French and that she was spiraling toward her demise.

I was mesmerized by all of this intrigue and still not believing that I was part of it. *Am I really living this adventure—or is this a nightmare of epic proportion?* As I slipped away, comforted by the warm fire and full belly, the snoring of my comrades allowed my temporary feeling of security to overtake my chronic paranoia.

Chirping birds and a babbling brook woke me gradually. My buddies still slept, so I took a moment to reflect. My life had never been so poignant and meaningful as that moment. I took advantage of a narcissistic thought and realized that all I had been had culminated in the here and now. The fact that I had been abandoned at a very young age, passed through countless relatives' homes, and been a burden to so many people during the Depression brought me to a sudden understanding of the fragility of family relationships. It took a war, a brush with death, and Frenchmen to bring these truths into my life. *I am changed forever. I will die for these men!*

I stripped down and jumped into the rushing brook. The cold blast cleared my head, and it was wonderful to be alive!

Rene said, "Eh, you good-for-nothin' Yankee pilot, where's our eggs and rashers? The first one up cooks breakfast! I like my eggs fried, and Armand wants his soft-boiled eggs served in a Spode cup. We want toast with clotted cream *s'il vous plait*! You Americans fly like birds—so walk on water and cook breakfast!"

No mercy for the merciless, I thought.

"Hold on. The cavalry is coming to save your French arses once again!"

We three knew that, without this banter, the journey would be dismal at best.

Fed, bathed, spit-shined, and ready for Pau, we were like children playing Robinson Crusoe looking for our next adventure.

We packed up what little food we had and left the cave on foot to Anzac. I was the only one to skip breakfast. *This is new territory for me. Murder with a switchblade?*

Armand reminded me that I was a murdering coward since I destroyed towns and villages and killed people without ever seeing their faces from the cockpit of my plane. *Touché! He not only knows how to kill with a knife—he knows how to twist it! He is right.*

I had been caught up in the fighter pilot mystique along with so many of my buddies that we did our killing job and never looked back. If any of us had stopped to think about our missions day after day, we would have been dysfunctional and no good for combat. *Maybe the dysfunction will haunt us in another life—away from this nightmare! I'm too exhausted to think about all of this.*

We stopped for the night near a small village and bedded down.

CHAPTER 14

BLEU SOLEIL

We knew something about our next contact: a couple who left their art gallery in Berlin for a buying trip to Paris. While there, they learned of a total ransacking of their gallery and home in Berlin. Nazi invaders were the perpetrators. There was no need to return. They funneled their way southwest toward the neutral border of Spain with the aim of helping the French Resistance cause. They had lost everything and were making a new start in their lives.

We walked along and marveled at the beautiful scenery. We approached the village of Pau and saw the masts of sailboats in the distance. We knew we were looking at the marina at Gare de Pau. We had not expected such a bucolic scene at a working harbor.

We had been briefed to watch for a thirty-foot sloop with a blue hull, aptly named *Bleu Soleil*. Our contacts would be aboard with their cairn terrier. *Since dogs are rarely seen on board, it should be an easy find.*

I was amazed to see so many boats in the marina—until I realized that political unrest probably kept mariners close at home. We climbed up on a small knoll and scanned the river. There were very few houses, but a number of fishing shacks dotted the landscape. We noted a small cabin with smoke rising from the chimney and a few gnarly-looking characters mending seine nets. Rene decided to reconnoiter and report back to us with a plan.

Armand and I hid under thickets of rosemary and waited.

Rene returned after finding our comrades.

The plan was to separate and meet up at the first shack. We would be provided with suitable sailing garb since our baggy peasant clothes would not fit the part of vacationing tourists.

Armand went to the fishing shack first, and I followed him after a short time, hoping not to be noticed. Rene had already been fitted out with nautical gear during his first visit with the fishermen. Armand and I took our turn at transforming ourselves into sailors.

The three of us met up together on the dock space allotted to *Bleu Soleil* and readied ourselves for the next leg of the journey.

Our new comrades revealed themselves gently. Rene, ever the master of control, approached the beautiful blue sloop with confidence and aplomb. A cairn terrier barked, and Lulu welcomed us aboard and took us to meet Captain Hans. We knew that our lives were in their hands. I was still the deaf-mute, which made my part in the play very easy.

Armand cast off the lines, and the three of us were once again at the mercy of our captors. Even though we were in the Gave de Pau River, we were in water affected by the ocean tides. We sailed with the outgoing tide for a few hours toward a peninsula, which soon revealed a deep cove nestled against a backdrop of pine trees. A chalet came into view, and it looked like it belonged in a movie. We docked quickly, disembarked, and trudged up the moss-covered hill to our new home. We embraced the cover of the chalet.

We were greeted by the warmth of a woodstove and the smell of a wonderful stew. Crusty bread with butter waited on the long table. We were invited to sit and share wine, cheese, and stories. At last, I found my voice and thanked my hosts for their hospitality and devotion to the cause. We climbed the ladder to the sleeping loft and fell easily into the feather beds.

Morning came too soon, but the coffee jolted mind and spirit. We would be taking the bus from here to Oloron, a distance of thirty-two kilometers, where we would connect with our alpine guide. We were assured by our hosts that this travel plan would be safe if we followed our usual protocol: Rene and I together and Armand in the background.

We changed into our travel clothes, returning physically—if not mentally—to our peasant disguises. Laden with food and wine, we were surprised by the wonderful gift of hand-knit wool socks from Lulu. She explained that keeping feet dry while crossing the mountains was a real necessity for survival; frostbite was a threat in the wet spring climate. She told us to put dry socks on in the morning and place the worn, damp socks from the day before on each shoulder directly on our skin, under our coats. Our body heat would dry the socks as we climbed. Dry socks for the next day for us. This was a valuable lesson that we practiced along our journey. *No frostbite!*

We packed up our gear, bade our new friends a heartfelt goodbye, and headed down the road toward the bus to Oloron.

CHAPTER 15

BLUE SMOKE

On the bus, we mapped our next stop through a small village near Oloron, our last stopping point before the winding ascent up the mountain. There, we were to meet up with our guide and secure our travel with supplies.

Again, the Catholic church came to our aid. The Resistance had done its homework well, and the local priest, Father Fraichette, was our savior. We were escorted into the bowels of the church, fed, and welcomed into the sanctity of religion once more. As an atheist, I was beginning to doubt my past philosophy, but I would save those thoughts for another day—when I could assess my transgressions in a less dramatic environment.

***

In the morning, Rene, Armand, and I awoke to the sound of wood being chopped and the smell of breakfast cooking over a wood fire just outside our shelter near the church.

The aroma of freshly brewed coffee jolted us from a deep sleep. We dressed quickly, scrambled toward the fire, and expected to see a worker from the priest's kitchen. The food simmered away with no apparent chef in sight.

Off in the distance, we saw a tall lad wielding an ax. He was clearly the source of the noise. We huddled around the fire, poured coffee, and waited for the woodchopper to join us. As we drank our second cup of coffee, the chopping stopped. The lad, armed with kindling wood, ambled toward us with a small terrier leading the way.

Father Fraichette appeared and said, "Let me introduce you to your guide."

We watched as this tall, slightly built person approached us, like an apparition stepping out of the swirling, blue campfire smoke. The terrier announced the arrival of both. We stood in anticipation of meeting this person of interest—in whose hands we would be placing our lives.

As the lad approached, he removed an alpine cap, and long flowing blonde hair tumbled everywhere. The long strides shortened, and she held out her hand and said, "I am Sofia Gold. We will be traveling companions to Pamplona."

I was aghast at the thought of this beautiful woman being our guide over the Pyrenees. I thought briefly of hugging her as I would have hugged a sister, but she held out her hand and systematically shook and clasped our hands with a rough-skinned handshake that almost brought each of us to our knees. This woman was not only beautiful; she was strong and resolute. One look into those steely hazel eyes, and I knew she was our salvation. With a quick glance at my comrades, I knew that they knew it too!

I shot a quick glance at Father Fraichette as he snickered in the sleeve of his cassock.

We settled around the fire and filled our metal plates with sausages, eggs, and thick bread, compliments of our priest friend. The conversation was easy and congenial.

"Sofia, how many trips to Pamplona have you made in your life?" Father Fraichette asked the question that we all wanted to ask but did not dare.

"Priest, more trips than you could even imagine. Your fat belly would exist only in your dreams if you had ever kept up with all of us. But keep the faith— you are doing your share in the fight. Your French comrades will continue to feed the need of the Resistance through your church, and that is a worthwhile cause for which we are all thankful."

I felt reassured that this choice of guide would serve us well, and I thought that we must look like a happy family laughing, joking, and flinging bits of food to her dog.

After breakfast, we washed the utensils in the stream. Sofia disappeared to assemble the gear and ready us for the trip. As Rene, Armand, and I finished the chores, Father Fraichette briefed us about our guide.

Sofia was the daughter of a wealthy Russian family who was vacationing near the Black Sea in 1917. When the Bolshevik uprising broke out, her parents were killed. Her great-uncle, Boris Gold, rescued her as an infant and smuggled her in a duffel bag and escaped on foot through Turkey. They sailed across the Mediterranean to Spain and eventually made their home near Eugi, Spain, where her uncle still lives. The neutrality of Spain keeps them safe—for now.

"I believe her home in the mountains will be one of your stops," continued the priest. "She was educated by her uncle and is well versed in history, finance, and language. In addition to speaking Russian, French, German, Spanish, and English, she is an expert skier, naturalist, and mountaineer. You are in good hands, my friends."

I was again impressed by the ability of the Underground to connect us with people of different backgrounds from all over Europe. Each was devoted to a common cause: freedom from oppression.

We packed up our gear and waited for our leader. Sofia appeared with all her gear secured to her back. I was taken aback when I noticed she wore the classic L.L. Bean Maine Hunting Shoe. The boots were very high and laced with leather thongs that held heavy wool socks tucked into green wool pants. She wore layers of woolen garments, and an outer-waxed jacket completed the wardrobe and offered protection from the most perilous weather that this environment could bestow. As she worked at packing the gear, I noticed that the right side of her jacket had caught up on a sidearm in a leather holster at her hip. She was carrying a Colt .45. She noticed my long stare, but she went about her tasks without comment.

I had never seen a woman carrying a sidearm of any type—let alone a Colt .45! I stared at the weapon, and for a brief moment, I thought of asking her if she had ever fired it. As our eyes met, I thought the better of it. She could really project her answers to questions before they were asked.

Feeling the awkwardness of the moment, I quickly looked away from the gun and down at her footgear. "Your boots were made near my hometown in Maine," I said.

She gave me a nod and did not seem impressed with my observation. She looked down at my well-worn leather boots and said, "Why doesn't your government issue these boots to soldiers if the boots are made in America? It would seem beneficial to all."

"If I had known that I was going to be shot down and have to climb these mountains, I would have bought the boots myself," I explained.

She laughed and circled her head with her index finger in the universal language of crazy.

We were becoming a team with a new leader, and now Rene was second-in-command.

CHAPTER 16

LAVENDER BLUE

We continued to pack and assess our clothing needs.

Father Fraichette appeared with three well-worn waxed jackets and tossed them in our direction. "Wear them well, boys, and return them to Sofia in Pamplona. She will bring them back here to be made ready for our next pilgrims on the trail to salvation over the mountain."

Rene and Armand chuckled quietly in the background. Not being of the Catholic persuasion, I was baffled. "What's going on? A French inside joke?" I asked.

"Earle, my son," the priest continued, " as the temporary keeper of your soul on this journey through hell, I am forced to inform you of your decision to make a pilgrimage, along with your companions, to the Basque town of Saint-Jean-Pied-de-Port to revel in the fine old chapel there. Many pilgrims have gone before you to Eglise Notre Dame de l'Assomption, which is where many souls have been enriched and delivered from sin during this forthcoming celebration of Easter."

"Well, I'll be jiggered! Who knew that I would come to the house of the Lord like this! The joke is on me! Praise the Lord—and pass the ammunition!"

The others rolled their eyes in disapproval of my blasphemy. *Maybe I was too cavalier about religion. Who knows? Maybe I will become a believer. If this war hasn't made me one yet, there's probably little hope for my conversion. On the other hand, maybe calling down the deities for my own entertainment was a bad idea. Never tempt fate!*

We loaded ourselves with our gear and all the food we could muster from the priest, which consisted of mostly nonperishable items: potatoes, hard bread, hard-boiled eggs, apples, raisins, cheese, and parsnips, my personal favorite. Water would be plentiful along the way. We stuffed our pockets with all that they could hold. We would restock en route per arrangements made in advance by the Resistance in Oloron.

Sofia said, "The weather in the southwestern area of the Pyrenees can be inclement in April—with wind, rain, and cold. We dress in layers, allowing us to add and subtract items as needed. Rain will be our nemesis. Okay, mes amis, let's be on our way."

We waved farewell to our priest and his fellow Underground associates, and we were really on our way. It was the first time since being shot down in March that I felt I was going back to England.

Carpets of French lavender engulfed us as we walked the winding dirt path that led us from about eleven hundred meters in elevation to about sixteen hundred meters just over a week. We would follow this less-traveled route to avoid any German contact, and the gradual ascent would allow us to climb gradually without terrible fatigue. The clean air was wonderful, and we were up for the challenge. We walked along briskly. Soon shadows began to lengthen, and a chill was in the air.

As we walked, the terrier began rooting in the dead leaves and barking. Sofia disappeared with the dog. Just as we were wondering what the ruckus was about, they both returned.

Sofia's hat was full of wild mushrooms. "We eat well tonight! There is a cave up ahead. Let's make camp and dinner!"

"Oui," we all said.

Rene was not much of a dog lover, but he allowed that Sofia's terrier was good for something after all. We went about our campsite duties and built a fire. While supper cooked, we gathered boughs of cedar to line our bedding. We rested well.

We were up with the birds and had cold tea and bread. We packed and cleaned up the campsite while Sofia engaged in a review of a regional map, which included the Basque area of southwest France and northern Spain.

As she finished her map review, we gathered around for her plan.

"Tonight, we'll camp near a small commune near Barcus. We need to figure out the security of the Camino Santiago's halfway point. Spring is a popular time for Catholics. They use this route to make pilgrimages to churches in Spain during Easter. Sometimes Nazi spies are placed in that area—among the pilgrims—to ferret out Resistance fighters. When we determine if it is safe, we will head to Saint-Jean-Pied-de-Port in France. From there, we will travel south to my family's home near Eugi, Spain. Uncle Boris is part of the Resistance movement and feels safer there than in France. He will have critical information about when descent down the other side is safe to tackle. We must be on guard at all times—and be careful about what we say to anyone."

Rene added, "When we come upon anyone, we are on a family pilgrimage, and Earle is deaf and dumb since he speaks French like a dog! You Yanks always take the easy way out, eh?"

Rene's old self resurfaced. He had been on his best behavior around our guide, and Armand and I wondered how long it would continue.

We headed out into the mountain fog. The cold fog reminded me of Debden, and I wondered if my buddies remembered me. *They would never guess that I am a Catholic mute crossing the Pyrenees with a bunch of Frenchmen and a beautiful woman!*

CHAPTER 17

BLUE MIST

We marched single file through hedges of abandoned grapevines and prickly gorse bushes that tore into exposed skin or rough clothing. The climb was different from before. The trails were treacherous with abrupt changes in footing. Caliche was as hard as concrete, and piles of slippery moss made hazardous footing conditions that caused us to slow our pace. We did not need to break any bones.

We'd been at it for about eight kilometers and needed a break. We basked in the warm April sun and filled canteens from an alpine stream. Snacks came out, and we rested.

Sofia told us that we needed to press on until dark. We were expected in Barcus that night, and our contacts had arranged a meal and shelter in a private chapel. She added, "We will be safe and well-fed. Anyone wishing to back out now and return to Oloron only gets to take the parsnips!"

Rene replied, "You really know how to inspire the troops with your flowery imagery. Looks like we don't have any deserters at this point! Saddle up, cowboys—and mind the trail, boss!"

She smiled and retorted, "Rene has seen too many John Wayne movies, and my goal is to make sure we live to see more!"

She can give as good as she gets!

We lumbered up the path for few more hours and began to feel fatigued. The air was thinner with every step, and it was an exhausting effort. Evening was approaching.

Up ahead, we saw a donkey led by an old woman.

Sofia signaled for us to drop behind her, and she put her right hand inside her jacket on her right hip. She was taking no chances.

We followed her lead and placed our hands on our own firearms.

As we neared each other, the woman announced, "This is my donkey, Paco."

That was the secret code. We all breathed a sigh of relief.

We followed Paco over the next grade to a chapel in a thicket of cedar trees that was hiding our new friends. Warm greetings, hugs, bottles of wine, and a feast kept us busy until midnight.

We bedded down inside the stone chapel on our potato sacks filled with fragrant cedar boughs and fell into deep sleep. *There's no insomnia here.*

With no time to waste in the morning, we drank hot tea, ate bread and cheese, gathered up our fresh food stores, which had been provided by the locals, and headed off again.

The four of us left the village of Barcus, headed toward Basque country, and began our gradual descent down the hilly Mediterranean terrain. Sofia entertained us with a constant travelogue of what she considered to be important information. As the three of us kept up with her, we were left winded and quiet.

Her love for the area was obvious. "We are in the Pyrenees-Atlantiques. West of us is the Midi-Pyrenees, an area where Basque people settled, farmed, and raised sheep and cows. They are hardworking, trustworthy people. They are good stewards of the land and sea. They fish and have played a big part in the colonization of the New World. Remember, if you want to learn about the world, go to war!"

We all sent a Bronx cheer and thumbs-down her way!

The day passed quickly, and as darkness fell, we looked for a place to stop. We found a small cave and settled in. We fell into our tasks and bedded down for the night.

Sofia said, "Tomorrow, my friends, we will have hot baths and sleep in feather beds in my uncle's home. We will stay for a few days and regroup before the big push, eh? My uncle will be glad to have the company, and you will find him most fascinating."

I nodded off and dreamed of a chateau in the Pyrenees.

***

We woke to the sound of people tramping through dry brush and leaves. We dressed and left the cave, not knowing what to expect. We were still technically in France and wary of being caught. Freedom was in Spain, and Spain was not yet under our feet.

We could not see our visitors, but we could hear deep masculine voices speaking in German and French. We built a fire and made tea—as though all was well—but were on guard.

I was sweating like a stuck pig, but Sofia was cool as a cucumber as she spoke French to Armand and Rene. That was my cue to be the deaf-mute.

Our visitors numbered five: four men and a teenage boy. I retreated into the cave in case the boy wanted to have a conversation with me.

My companions played the good hosts and invited them for a hot drink, and they accepted.

Shit! Now what do I do?

As Rene poured tea, Sofia came in to check on me. "Stay in here," she said quietly. "I will tell them you are ill. One of them gives me an uneasy feeling, but we will be we convivial and then allow them to go on ahead. They are probably on a pilgrimage since this is Easter week." She returned to the group, and they all spoke in hushed voices and finished their drinks.

At last, the intruders stood up to leave and shook hands all around. They said their goodbyes and continued on their way.

Armand stuck his head in the cave and told me the coast was clear.

The group was on their way to Camino de Santiago in Spain. We were on the same route, but we had different goals in mind.

Armand said, "Rene and I agree with Sofia that one man in the group seemed to set off an alarm. He spoke German, and he queried us about developments in the war. We, of course, pled ignorance and allowed that we were on a journey to visit family in the mountains. He accepted our story. The pack leader continually leered at Sofia. I saw Rene's jaw tighten each time he looked her way. They're gone now. No worries, mate!"

We gave each other knowing looks. We had been warned, in Oloron, about German intelligence officers who mingled with peasants on pilgrimages in order to extract information about French or German Jews who were escaping into Spain.

We must be on our game and not let our guard down. Any of these pilgrims could be looking for escapees like us. Hopefully, we fit the profile of a happy family group who is headed to their family for the Easter holiday.

CHAPTER 18

BLUE TWILIGHT

We decided to lay low until dawn the next day to give our pilgrim friends a day's walk ahead of us. We needed a break and a good night of undisturbed sleep.

Rain moved in, and the wind was a cold blast from the north. We spent most of the day in the cave. For our main meal, we fried up potatoes, onions, and parsnips.

As we reminisced about the taste of meat, we noticed Sofia was missing. Probably gone to the loo, we surmised.

After an hour had passed, we began to worry. Just as Rene was readying himself as a search party, she appeared with two fat rabbits slung over her shoulder. They were dressed out, skewered, and ready for the hot coals. "Couldn't wait for you guys to feed us now, could I? Enjoy!"

We praised her skill with her slingshot!

A renaissance woman to be sure.

We feasted and hit the sack early.

***

We woke at daybreak to the sound of people stomping through the brush. We knew the foot traffic along the trail to Santiago would be busy with Easter Sunday ahead.

We broke camp and hit the trail toward our evening destination: Uncle Boris and his chateau! The smell of clean mountain air refreshed us. We saw recent tracks all around, and broken twigs and small branches littered the ground.

Rene said, "Many foot soldiers walked through here last night on the way to salvation, eh, Yankee? I trust you all slept well without being disturbed. Good thing Sofia and I kept you all safe!"

I said, "We slept well because we knew you were on watch, my good man. Armand and I will return the favor someday!"

We were feeling more and more at ease with Sofia, and I noticed that the banter made her smile. She hid her smile by pulling her hat down over one side of her face. She probably thought we wouldn't notice, but we did.

***

Up at daybreak, we packed all the gear. We all had lighthearted feelings and embraced the day's adventure. No fire—just fresh stream water and light fare to eat. After all, tonight we would dine at a real table and sit in chairs at the family compound. We had been lucky so far! Sunshine and soft breezes were our inspiration to push onward through the Basque region.

Sofia said, "We should be able to cover at least sixteen kilometers today and arrive on the southernmost side of my home, on the downward slope of the mountain, before supper. Less than eighty kilometers from there, and Pamplona is ours, my fine-feathered friends. I am proud of all of you. My reputation as an alpine guide is still secure, but I am not so sure that I have done much to improve your chronic lack of personal hygiene."

"Aw, you really know how to hurt our feelings," said Rene. "We are no dirtier than the pilgrims on the trail. We keep in character of sinners, suffering for our sins and transgressions to avoid suspicion. With that said, I will command Armand and Earle to stuff lavender and rosemary into their jackets to lessen the aroma."

"Are there enough wildflowers in the Pyrenees?" she retorted.

We rested and marveled at the beauty in the world. We watched as soldiers of the Lord passed by, using their walking sticks to flatten brush along the pathway. We nodded, kept silent, and pretended to nap.

I said, "So, what is the fascination with this particular journey to Pamplona, anyway? Anyone here know? Since you all seem to be somewhat God-fearing people, anybody here willing to educate this Yankee foot soldier?"

Sofia rose to the challenge and said, "There are indeed many stories about this trail. This version, told by my uncle, credits the Virgin Mary with the holy burden placed upon her by God to bring pilgrims to worship. Mary appeared to a shepherd, tending his flock on this road, and asked him to build a church to provide shelter and respite for the weary people. When a shepherd asked where the chapel should be built, Mary pulled a slingshot from her garment and shot a stone at a faraway hillside. That was the site of a church that was built in what is now Pamplona, Spain. The Cathedral of Santiago de Compostela is that church. It is also said that the remains of Saint James are buried near the site. Many believe that walking such a great distance to visit this shrine—while relinquishing creature comforts—brings them closer to God and puts them on a fast track to heaven. Uncle Boris does not believe in any of this and insists that he makes his own heaven and hell on earth! I agree with my uncle's philosophy, but I always carry my slingshot in case I need food—not the location of a chapel that needs to be built."

We collectively concluded that this conversation should continue while drinking large quantities of alcohol with Uncle Boris. It seemed we were kindred spirits after all!

CHAPTER 19

BLUE CHATEAU

We were refreshed and ready to continue on our next layover at the chateau. This segment would be a push, but we were up to the task.

We started out single file with Sofia in the lead.

Rene and Sofia walked together and chatted quietly.

Armand snickered at the blooming friendship between them, rolled his eyes, and said, "We knew this would happen, right?"

I replied, "Yes, we did, mon ami. I guess that means we must console ourselves in our loneliness."

We marched on and passed more pilgrims, but we kept our focus on the journey. We took a short break for lunch, and before we knew it, Sofia pointed out a beautiful house in the distance. As she shared her binoculars with us, we were impressed with the beauty of the wooden chateau, which was crowned by a blue tile roof that shone in the late afternoon sunshine. We veered off the main path and started a slight ascent toward the compound. A few outbuildings nestled among the trees and the whole scene reminded me of a fairy tale. We had arrived.

The large wooden door—carved with animals of the forest—imparted a childlike feeling of nostalgia. As we approached, the door was flung open, and a giant man with a shock of white hair and a long beard roared a hearty welcome.

Sofia rushed to him, and they hugged as though they would never let go.

After introductions were made, we entered the great hall, which was strewn with wool rugs and dogs. The dogs barked and jumped with reckless abandon as they greeted us and Sofia's truffle-rooting terrier.

"So, you have brought us another batch of refugees, my dear?" Boris turned to us and said, "We like to know that even though our efforts seem small indeed, we help good people escape the Nazi war machine … a machine that kills, maims, and plunders—all in the name of the Third Reich! Welcome to our home! Our house is your house!"

Uncle Boris certainly is a force to contend with—just like his niece!

"Ingrid, come and show our new friends to their rooms. You must make yourselves comfortable. Each room has its own bathtub, so you must avail yourselves of a deep soak before dinner. Sofia and I will catch up on news while you refresh yourselves."

It looked as though there was a conspiracy to get us bathed and shaved! Even the dogs whined and avoided us!

Ingrid scurried up the winding staircase and waved for us to follow her. She took each of us into our own suite, and fresh white towels waited on the beds.

I quickly ran hot water in the tub and slid in up to my neck in steamy, lavender-scented bubbles. I shaved and found casual clothing laid out on the bed. I was the only one without a wardrobe. After being shot down, I didn't take time to pack before bailing out. The others had civvies and were prepared to meet their social obligations.

I headed down the stairs into the great hall of dogs, and an open door led me toward a quiet conversation. I entered a large room lined with massive bookshelves that reached from floor to ceiling. I wondered how long it would take someone to read all those books. Rene and Armand sat around a large fireplace, enjoying the warmth and comfort of red velvet chairs.

Rene said, "Well, Earle, we were about to see if you had drowned in that tub. Too much cleanliness will ruin your reputation."

"I'll try to do better in that regard," I answered.

Boris opened a large cabinet and brought out his favorite scotch. "I trust you will join me in toasting your arrival to my humble home?"

We gladly obliged him, clinked our glasses together, and drank to good health.

"Where's our Sofia? Come, woman, and drink with us!" Boris commanded.

Sofia appeared in the doorway in a long green velvet dressing gown and gold slippers. Her hair was down to her waist and tied loosely to one side with a ribbon. The three of us were tongue-tied and unable to swallow. *She is beautiful!*

"My favorite scotch, Uncle. Make mine a double. After all, I have put up with them for many weeks and deserve a reward." She winked at us and laughed.

While we were composing ourselves, Boris handed her a scotch.

She immediately tossed it back, put down her glass, and asked for another.

We were impressed to say the least.

"My niece takes after her old uncle in the liquor department. Who ever heard of Russians drinking Glenlivet! We are supposed to drink vodka! *Nostrovia!*" bellowed Boris.

Ingrid appeared in the doorway and announced that dinner was on the table.

We followed the wonderful aroma to the dining room and sat down at the table.

Boris sat at the head of the table, and Sofia sat at the opposite end. Ingrid sat to the right of Boris. The implication was that she was his partner.

Food was plentiful: wild boar, fresh greens, and beans and rice—and no parsnips. The conversation was lively, and wine flowed out of crystal decanters. Dessert was chocolate cake followed by espresso laced with cognac and whipped cream.

Rene, Armand, and I cleared the table and helped in the kitchen. The three of us washed and dried the dishes and pans like brothers helping their mother at home. It was a good feeling.

CHAPTER 20

LAPIS BLUE

We stepped outside the kitchen door and checked out the night sky. The April night was full of creature sounds all around us. Pond frogs sang their mating songs, and owls hooted their hollow, throaty sounds, which echoed in the dark. Animal eyes peered at us through the trees and were soon revealed as belonging to the family dogs. They came bounding at us in all sizes and shapes. They wagged their tails and jumped on us.

Sofia said, "Uncle has summoned us to the library for rumination and a glass of port. Any volunteers? Ingrid has retired, and as expected, he is in conversation mode. He gets lonely here when I am away, and we must oblige him."

"Lead on, milady. We are at your beck and call!"

We followed her through the great hall and into the library. Dogs were now laid out every which way in front of the fire, soaking in the heat.

"Join me, my friends, in a glass of port and a cigar!" commanded Boris.

Sofia poured the wine and passed a box of the finest Cuban cigars. She clipped the ends with a cutting tool, lit up each smoke, and handed them out before lighting her own.

I'd never seen a woman smoke a cigar, and by the looks on the faces of Rene and Armand, they hadn't either.

The conversation flowed, the wine flowed, and we got to know and understand the past travails of the Gold family in Russia. Boris recounted how, as wealthy Russian Jews, the Gold family was a target of the Bolsheviks. As the family tried to escape from Russia in 1917, Sofia's parents were killed, but Uncle Boris and infant Sofia survived. Boris managed to hide Sofia in a duffel bag and escaped to the family's summer home near the Black Sea. The little family eventually found its way across Spain and into the Pyrenees mountains near the border of France.

"Enough of our plight, Uncle. Here we are with dear friends—in our safe place."

Boris countered, "Yes, my dear, you are right again! But please indulge me for a few more minutes as I tell them about our famous library."

"You will anyway—no matter what I say," she said with a disgruntled sigh.

Boris was now engaged in full-disclosure mode. "Now that we have become trusted comrades in fighting of the enemy, I must show you how we have managed to live here for all these years with only a modest income earned from my farm and tutoring local children."

He motioned for us to follow him into his library. Our full attention was his as he drew back a massive tapestry from an oak-paneled wall, which revealed many drawers made of exotic wood and brass knobs inlaid with lapis lazuli. The light from the fireplace danced off the brass and blue stone, casting shadows around the room.

"Come here, my friends, and I will show you!"

We three gathered around him, and as he opened a middle drawer, we gasped in wonder.

The drawer was brimming with gold coins of all denominations, gold bullion, and gold trinkets in the form of chains and bracelets. We stood amazed at the sight and were speechless.

He slid open another drawer that was filled with tiny velvet bags. "Hold out your hand, Earle." He poured the contents into my palm, and I cupped my palm to catch the diamonds as they tumbled out of the pouch. He opened another bag, and colored gems—emeralds, sapphires, and amethyst—filled Rene's palm. Armand was the next recipient, and strands of pearls spilled into his hand.

Boris chuckled at our faces. "I brought most of this with me when we left Russia. Our family accumulated this wealth over many generations of serving the Romanovs. It was common practice to bury wealth around the family estates and, most commonly, underneath outhouses. That secret was closely guarded in a place that most avoided. Only farmhands visited out of necessity." He looked around and added, "Note that Sofia is absent because she knows what I am about to say." Pointing to the diamonds in my hand, he said, "These gems are the shithouse diamonds! I went back to retrieve the jewels in 1938, before this war. Even though the Bolsheviks hadn't discovered them in 1918, I was not sure whether the Germans would find them this time."

While we ogled the gems, he allowed that the place of their confinement was, indeed, a secure spot. Boris returned the treasures back to their hiding places and secured the tapestry. "This calls for more drink and conversation," he roared.

This guy is inexhaustible, I thought.

We all returned to the dining room and rejoined Sofia.

Boris poured another round of port and said, "Most of us believe that war is a terrible waste of human life and resources. I tend to see war as an opportunity to establish new ideas and a chance to hone skills on how to make order out of chaos. Granted, this all comes with great cost and sacrifices by everyone, but perhaps, for future insight, we can learn how to avoid these confrontations in the first place.

"Diplomacy is key along with religious tolerance, but fat chance of that happening! Different religious philosophies—or lack thereof, by many—is the stickler. Famine, drought, disputes over boundaries, and poverty are constants around the world that will ensure the security of war."

"Enough, dear uncle! We have had enough of your wine-induced philosophical observations! Let our guests retire while they can still walk!" admonished Sofia.

We said our good nights and thanked her for getting us off the hook and releasing us from expressing a difference of opinion with our host. After all, a wealthy Russian aristocrat probably saw the world differently than us peasants.

"Uncle likes to throw out the bait! He does not believe half of what he says. He just wants spirited conversation. Pay him no mind."

Sofia's words comforted us. I was relieved to learn this. It would be hard to understand why anyone with such a harsh view of the world would spend his own money to help the French Resistance.

We trundled off to bed in anticipation of a wonderful rest.

CHAPTER 21

GOODBYE BLUES

We spent a few more days with the Gold family. The time passed quickly as we did chores and small projects around the compound. Boris appreciated the extra help, and we were happy to oblige and show our gratitude for the fine meals and hospitality.

Our last night with our new friend was somewhat emotional for all of us. Armand and I knew we would not be back there ever again, and things would never be the same.

Rene would continue shuffling humanity from France through the mountains as long as the war continued, and Sofia would continue funneling people into the neutrality of Spain and on to their destinations.

Ingrid and Boris put on a great feast on our last evening: spring lamb, farm-grown vegetables, bread, cheeses of all kinds, and thick cream on berries and cake for dessert. The wine flowed. We feasted outside under strings of lights rigged up by Rene and Sofia. Some local Basques joined us for the feasting and then serenaded us with their songs and guitars. All too soon, the evening was over. When the guests departed, we turned in.

Thoughts of tomorrow brought sad dreams.

***

In the morning, we were up with the chickens and down to the kitchen where Ingrid and Sofia were cooking breakfast.

Sofia said, "Uncle is collecting leftovers from our meal last night to take on our journey. There is plenty left in the larder, and we have miles yet to go."

As Rene, Armand, and I ate, Sofia briefed us like a drill sergeant. "We can be in Roncesvalles in a few days, but we have some bad news and good news to consider! Our climb will be rough going. We will ascend a few thousand meters through dense forest. The good news is that most of the pilgrims will have already passed by and are at their appointed destinations. After reaching Roncesvalles, we will descend the mountain for the next few days. Traveling downhill can be treacherous because many deep crevices are hidden by rocks and fallen trees. We'll be fine as long as we pay attention. I have traveled this many times and have suffered no more than a mosquito bite. We will pick up a bus to Pamplona, after passing through Eugi, in Spain. Total distance is about sixty-five kilometers. Any questions so far?"

We allowed that we had heard enough and needed to get to it. We packed up our gear and shared heartfelt hugs with Boris, Ingrid, and their staff. I pulled out my gold francs to repay our host, which I thought was protocol by military standard, but Boris refused payment from me.

"My son, when Sofia leaves you in Pamplona, you may give her your gold. She will add it to the coffers in the headquarters in Oloron. This is how it is done. Keep a few coins for a bullfight and tapas in Spain. You might have to wait for weeks in Pamplona for messages to get back to your military base as to your whereabouts."

As tears welled up in my eyes, I said, "Many thanks for your wonderful hospitality and generosity toward us. I will never forget you or this place."

We all hugged each other, picked up our gear, and waved goodbye.

As we looked back at Boris and Ingrid in front of their chalet, Boris said, "Never forget the shithouse diamonds, mes amis."

CHAPTER 22

LITTLE BLUE AND WHITE LIES

We trundled on as we had done before with our usual chatter and recounts of funny stories from our visit. We ascended the mountain as the late April sun rose high in the brilliant blue sky.

Trees provided refreshing shade as we picked our way up the incline. According to our guide, Uncle Boris's compound was about twenty-seven hundred meters above sea level. We would climb to about thirty-two hundred meters, reach Roncesvalles on the Spanish side of the Pyrenees, and descend sixteen hundred meters to Eugi. All in all, it would be quite a trip with many ups and downs to break the monotony of the walk. This was a longer escape route, but it was not widely monitored by the German army. Therefore, it was safer for us.

Along the way, a few hardy souls waved to us from the doorways of their hovels. It was best to keep to ourselves. As we passed, we commented on the great weather that had been following us. We pushed on while given the chance.

We bedded down at twilight in a cave covered with moss and wildflowers, and we allowed ourselves quiet reflection as we snuggled down for the night.

Sofia remarked, "You all thought this would be an excursion over meadows and brooks, but now you know the simple truth. If I had told you all of this at the start, you might have balked at the harshness of the climb and the elevation. Now you understand how easy this has been so far."

Rene said, "Any other little tidbits of information to share with us?"
Sofia just yawned, and no answer was forthcoming.
We didn't want to know anyway.

***

We were up at daybreak for the usual drill: we ate, packed up, and left.
Clouds were beginning to roll in, but we pressed on once more. We hoped to spend the night in an inn or a hostel in a village near Roncesvalles.

CHAPTER 23

BLUE MARIPOSA

May 1944

We had walked nearly thirty-eight kilometers in three days since we left the blue chateau on the mountain. We were ready for a hotel and a real meal.

Sofia announced, "There's a small inn up ahead on the River Urhobo where we can spend the night. It's not fancy, but it will meet our needs with baths, beds, and food. I've stayed there many times during crossings to and from Spain."

I said, "Sounds great to me. Would you guys prefer a cave and bread or a hot meal and a sheet?"

Rene and Armand grunted their approval.

We walked a short distance and saw a beautiful stream winding its way toward a white stucco building with a red-tiled roof covered with blue butterflies.

As we got closer, we could see people drinking wine and listening to flamenco guitar music at bistro tables. *We really are in Spain!* We found a table for four and unloaded our packs under trees.

"I'll reserve rooms for the night, and we'll let Earle pay the bill tomorrow, eh?" Rene announced.

"Happy to do so at any cost, my friend!" I replied.

Rene headed into the inn, and we ordered wine.

I got an uncomfortable feeling as I noticed a familiar group near our table. Not wanting to create feelings of paranoia, I still felt obligated to share my concern with my friends. "Do not turn your heads, but I think the men we met along the trail to the chateau are seated behind us. I remembered that one had a German accent. He made me uncomfortable, and he didn't seem like a peasant traveling to gain redemption."

Rene returned from the inn and announced that we had lucked out. He had procured the last three rooms.

"Well, someone will have to double up," Armand surmised.

"No worries—Sofia and I have it figured out!" Rene stated.

Armand and I whistled a long, low, breathy sound followed by a series of tongue clicks.

Sofia looked unflapped and sipped her wine. We ordered tapas to munch along with our wine and watched as a troupe of gypsies performed a folk dance.

Sofia removed her vest, and I noticed no sidearm on her hip. She caught my glance and nodded toward her duffel bag, which was covering the Colt .45.

We clapped, sang, and enjoyed the festivities. Rene and Sofia got up and danced to the haunting music, moving their bodies together as though they were one person.

I nudged Armand and pointed to her western boots. "They look like the genuine article, slanted heels and pointed toes ... probably custom jobs. Probably made from snake or lizard, big bucks."

"She wears them well, mon ami, n'est pas?"

As we watched the dancers, the German man ambled over to our table with his beer. He twirled Sofia's empty chair around, straddled it, leaned forward, and bent the back of the small chair forward with his large frame. "I see you have found your hearing and speech. Bon chance! This mountain air and religion can work miracles—even giving you an American accent!"

I broke out in a sweat and didn't know what to say or do. I did nothing. Deep down, I knew he had no jurisdiction over us in Spain, but I still worried.

Rene and Sofia appeared, and she stood in front of her chair and had a conversation in German with our unwelcome guest. The exchange got heated. He patted her bum, pulled her to him, and pointed to the dance floor.

Rene put his hand inside his coat.

Sofia lifted her right foot and drove the pointed toe of her boot up, underneath, and through the straw bottom of the chair. Since his legs were spread wide apart, it was clear that the boot hit its mark! He shot out of the chair and yelped like a wounded dog. Our German friend was last seen limping to his room at the inn.

I said, "That's what I call a self-sufficient woman. Remind me to stay on her good side!"

"Good advice for us all!" Rene said. "I was ready to draw my pistol and shoot the horny bastard to defend my woman's honor, but shooting him here would not have been good, given the commotion it would have caused. The world would not have missed another Nazi, me thinks."

We continued to drink wine and eat until long after midnight. After all, this would be over soon, and we would all be going our separate ways. These friendships would never be forgotten.

Armand and I found our way back to the inn and our own rooms. Rene and Sofia had departed the fix much earlier; they were smart! My head pounded, and I needed to hit the sack.

***

I woke with a start to the sound of church bells that called the faithful to Mass. *It must be Sunday.* I dressed and knocked on the doors of my friends, but there was no answer. They were already downstairs at the communal breakfast table.

As I approached them, Armand shouted, "We were beginning to wonder if you had died up there in your bed, but now, by looking at your bloodshot eyes, we think that you are nursing an overindulgence of some kind. Come sit with us and have the hair of the dog!"

A round of laughter and applause followed.

I bowed graciously and slipped in beside Rene.

My friends were drinking coffee laced with anise liqueur and eating omelets filled with cheese and vegetables.

I said, "I'll pass on the food and booze and do some quick swallows with coffee for now." After a gulp of coffee, I asked, "Has anyone seen our fellow pilgrim this morning?"

Sofia sipped her coffee, looked down at her turquoise boots, and replied, "Apparently, he is a late sleeper."

We all snickered and thought about how he must really be hurting this morning.

I settled the bill with the innkeeper, who was very happy with gold francs, the preferred exchange for hospitality.

CHAPTER 24

BLUE BUS TO PAMPLONA

With the end of our journey almost in sight, I packed up and eagerly anticipated the final leg—but not without trepidation. As we boarded the bus to Eugi, I felt quite secure in our successful escape from German control, but the ending remained nebulous.

Armand had a plan to fish off the coast of San Sebastian in Spain. He had a Hemingway obsession, and we were all okay with that. Sofia would head back to the chateau and then go on to Oloron to ferry more pilgrims across the mountain.

The mystery was Rene. He seemed changed—from the cavalier French Foreign Legionnaire to a more introspective man. *Is it love?*

Rene and Sofia were a unique couple. Their goals were the same, their politics were solid, and they were committed to the cause.

Me? My future as a flyer was probably over. Having been shot down, it would be unlikely that I would fly again. My connection with the Underground would make me a choice target for the enemy, assuming that I would divulge secrets to them. *Never, never, never! Pull out all my fingernails and toenails or electroshock me, but I will never disclose any information. I will suffer to the death!*

My fate would be to return to Debden to face the consequences of my superiors. They would ask me why I—an ace fighter pilot—was in the crosshairs of the guns of a Messerschmitt and enemy ground fire in the first place! *Bloody hell! They can bugger off!*

We left the infamous Mariposa Inn and headed southeast to catch the bus. We loaded onto the worn, tired, dilapidated old blue bus amid peasants with chickens stuffed in baskets, goats tethered to hooks in the back of the bus, and old men with produce wrapped in dirty blankets. We tried to assimilate, and I enjoyed the distraction.

The jolting ride kept me focused, and each pothole reminded me how lucky we were to have come so far on our journey.

We approached more densely populated villages as we descended into the valley. The lush Spanish countryside beckoned us into the soft veil of moss-covered stone walls, flowers that climbed up church steeples, hibiscus, and endless hedges of roses that filled the air with wonderful scent.

We stopped near a market that bustled with activity. Sofia had a brief discussion with the bus driver and ascertained that this was the end of the line. We had made it to Pamplona, Spain.

We grabbed our gear and headed to the Cathedral de Santa Maria. At the church, we would meet our liaison here in Pamplona.

The beautiful church wasn't hard to find—even for us. The distinctive Moorish architectural features and the crucifix on the dome fit the description that we were given by the Underground.

We headed up the steep steps and entered a world of quiet and calm. Votive candles flickered softly and reflected light that danced on the stained glass windows. We all genuflected and took seats together in the front pew—where we could see and be seen.

A few moments later, a tall man in a cassock appeared and motioned for us to follow him. We trusted him and walked single file down a dark passageway. No words were spoken.

Just as I was getting a strange feeling in my gut, the priest pushed through giant oak doors, and we all stepped into a room filled with men and women who stood up, applauded, and whistled. What a welcome to Pamplona! We learned that our arrival was later than expected, and there had been cause for worry.

Food was set out for all to enjoy. Amid great revelry, Father Shaw introduced us to the extended family of the French Resistance, about twenty people who had helped along the way.

A copy of my American passport, my military address in Britain, and my rank and serial number were presented to me. I cleared my throat and struggled to hold back my emotions, but my tears flowed, cleansing my whole being.

Through heartfelt sobs, I said, "How can I ever repay this group for returning my identity to me. I am no longer a deaf-mute Frenchman! Thank you for giving me back my life. I am humbled in your presence."

The collective voice responded, "Hear hear."

CHAPTER 25

GRAN HOTEL
LE PERLA

We collected our baggage and shook the hands of each new friend, followed by hugs and kisses on each cheek. These dedicated, passionate people volunteered their services for the cause of freedom. They conducted their secret business in the bowels of the church, which was where information about the war was gathered and dispersed. The group included Spaniards who made counterfeit identification papers and passports for almost anyone escaping persecution—anywhere in the world. These talented artists, printers, and chemists created documents that looked authentic and well used.

I slipped a handful of gold into the robe pocket of Father Shaw, and he nodded. "Thank you, my son."

"My great pleasure." I nodded and bowed my head to the group.

Father Shaw escorted us to a beautiful hotel across the city square. He said, "The concierge is expecting you and will honor your requests for accommodations. No money is expected since we all try to do what we can to keep Spain neutral. The presence of war heroes, like yourselves, in our city is much revered. We have known discord in our country too."

I was humbled by his remarks and said, "Father, you flatter me. I am no hero. I'm just a Yankee boy who wants to return to Britain in time for tea and scones someday. I am much obliged to you and your team."

Rene said, "Speak for yourself, mon ami. I, on the other hand, will accept the title of hero since I singlehandedly fought off a band of Romany gypsies who were trying to take advantage of my American pilot friend."

We all laughed as Rene took an exaggerated bow.

Father Shaw announced that he would see us in church on the morrow.

The four of us entered the hotel lobby and were handsomely rewarded for our lack of conveniences along the trail. The lobby was an assault on the senses. Baroque-style mirrors hung on the walls in sharp contrast to the flat, unidimensional, surreal images by Dali and Picasso.

Tapestries blinded us with their bold colors and shimmering threads reflected by the luminescent light from crystal chandeliers suspended from the vaulted ceilings. A giant fountain bubbled in the center of the room, acting as a pedestrian traffic circle and keeping incoming feet to the right and outgoing feet to left.

The concierge bowed, welcomed us to his hotel, and gave us keys to our rooms. He mentioned meeting with us in the morning and quickly disappeared. We found our rooms and said our good nights. Sleep beckoned.

***

I awoke to the crowing of roosters in the heart of Pamplona. *Who knew of this insult? No rest for the weary,* I thought. *Up and onward! I need to go over to the church to get details for how to get out of this country and home.*

Armand, Rene, and Sofia were sipping coffee on the edge of the fountain and perusing the hotel's art collection.

Rene said, "Welcome to our personal art gallery. I am not a student of art, but Sofia is well versed on the subject, compliments of Uncle Boris. I find Dali hard to take without at least two bottles of wine before viewing his distorted, delusional perspective on humanity. Dali is best viewed just before regurgitation ... or maybe after. That way, the mind is clear. What say you, my Yankee friend?"

"I say that having an opinion about art is personal. It's mine, and no one else has it. I will defer to your European education. Let's leave art, religion, and politics out of this—or I might have to challenge you to a duel."

"It would be a sad day for a duel, my friend. Your most worthy opponent is no other than Rene Chabot, l'enfant terrible of the elite special forces of my regiment!"

"Okay, okay. I acquiesce. You, sir, are my superior in this matter of dueling. On to the church and our future!" I said with tongue-in-cheek humor.

With a quick nod to the concierge and an implied guarantee that we would be right back,we headed to our friendly church across the square. The heavy oak doors were locked, which was very unusual for a Catholic church, especially in the morning. We were all overly suspicious of every detail about our mission.

As we were about to turn and go down the steps, the door swung open. A familiar face appeared, but it was not Father Shaw. A member of the Resistance group that had welcomed us the previous day invited us inside and explained that Father Shaw was buying our train tickets for the final leg of our journey. He explained that Armand and I would travel together to Villabona. Once there, Armand would catch a bus to San Sebastián, on the coast of Spain, and I'd continue to Bilbao by train, traveling south. In Gibraltar, I will be met by a transport plane—not a ship—that would return me to Debden.

Sounds easy. Not to worry!

My plan was to get to Britain, and someone else would have to fill in the blanks.

Father Shaw returned eventually, and the plan was hatched.

Rene and Sofia listened intently and took in all the information dispensed by the two priests. Everyone agreed that it was the best plan for getting me back to my unit in Britain and Armand to a safe place until the war ended.

Resistance people would get word to my unit that I had survived my plane crash and had walked out of France, across the Pyrenees, and into Spain. Upon my arrival in Gibraltar, the pilot of the transport plane would send a messenger to my base about our arrival time in Britain.

The two priests said, "Let's drink to the success of the plan!"

"Hear hear!" We lifted our glasses to each other.

CHAPTER 26

BLUE FUTURE

Rene, Sofia, Armand, and I headed back to our hotel in the late afternoon. A nap and a last meal together were part of the plan.

For me, sleep was impossible. I bathed, rounded up my clothes, packed up my kit, and went downstairs. The lobby was empty except for maids polishing the marble floor.

The concierge was busying himself with papers at his desk.

"I want to settle our bill since we all leave tomorrow," I said.

He replied, "My friend, there is no charge for your visit here. We are much honored to have you and your companions as guests."

I pondered my next move. *These Spaniards are easily offended.* "I am thinking that there is an orphanage connected with this church across the way. Please accept this donation and offer it to the children's fund. I insist that you take the coins as tokens of our gratitude. After all, where else could I have seen this wonderful artwork and dined in such surroundings? My conscience will be clear knowing that I have helped in some way."

The concierge answered, "Since you have put forth this offer so humbly, I will accept—with many thanks."

I wandered the halls of the hotel and admired the beautiful architecture, which had survived the Spanish Civil War. Among all the trappings were posters of local bullfights, including the names of the bulls and matadors. I was glad we were leaving in the morning and would have no time to view this blood sport.

The San Fermin Festival would begin in a few weeks, and people would come from all over the world. *Armand's heart will be broken. Too bad!*

I sat at the bar and waited for the siesta to end. The hotel was coming alive as patrons readied for a night of celebration.

I heard familiar voices, and my friends spotted me in the bar. *We all look like normal people*, I thought, *meeting for an evening of festivities.*

Rene and Armand looked crisp and clean in white shirts, bolo ties, and khakis.

Sofia looked ravishing in a long black skirt and white silk chemise. Her hair was loose and flowed down her back. She wore turquoise earrings and matching bracelets that jingled with each move of her suntanned arms.

"Hold out your hand," she said. "I don't want you to feel left out." She dropped a bolo tie into my palm. "Of course, while you all slept, I went shopping. Anyway, you all now have a memento of our trip together." She slid the tie over my head, and I caught a whiff of her lavender scent.

With a teasing grin, Rene said, "Earle wants to know what you are wearing on your feet—in case we need protection."

She yanked up her skirt and revealed the infamous turquoise and silver-toed boots!

We linked our arms together and headed out to the patio. Under the Spanish moon and stars, we ate and drank as though there would be no tomorrow. The food kept coming—along with champagne to clear our palates between courses. Cakes with berries, flan, and cheese platters completed our meal. Flamenco music and soulful singing voices filled us with a passion for these gypsy musicians.

Out of the corner of my eye, I saw Rene down on one knee in front of Sofia. I nudged Armand, and he winked at me. We couldn't hear what transpired, but judging by the looks on their faces, all was going well. Rene slipped a ring on her finger, and it fit perfectly! He then scooped her up in his arms and swung her around in a circle in time to the music.

Everyone clapped and wished them well. All too soon, we parted and headed back to our rooms. *Tomorrow will be a day unlike any other.*

In the morning, Armand, Rene, and I scurried to finish our toilet while we left Sofia in her room to dress for her wedding. We took our coffee and brioche over to our favorite seat on the lobby fountain. We teased Rene and tortured him with predictions of marital bliss and many babies. He took it all in stride.

Soon, our fourth soldier appeared in a long yellow silk dress and a lace mantilla held in place by a large silver comb. Her hair was piled high with tendrils around her face.

We were speechless.

"Just so your curiosity doesn't get the best of you, I *am* wearing them to my wedding." She poked her foot out from under her dress. *The turquoise boots!*

We all laughed at the same time.

Rene caressed her face. "Father Shaw is expecting us presently—so let's get this wedding started. Our two best men will pick your bouquet from the hotel garden, my darling girl."

We all picked the flowers and made a wedding bouquet of violets, daisies, and daffodils. Sofia picked three yellow roses and wound them into our bolo ties.

Perfect!

Father Shaw greeted us, and Rene and Sofia exchanged vows and became man and wife.

The massive church bells sounded their joy!

CHAPTER 27

BLUE WATERS OF SAN SEBASTIAN

Wedding vows exchanged between Rene and Sofia were sealed with a kiss. We trudged over to the hotel and found our bags waiting in the lobby.

We said our goodbyes to Father Shaw, and he left us with a blessing for our journey. Rene and Sofia hugged us, and we all told each other to keep in touch. *Who knows? I think it might happen.*

Armand and I needed to hurry to catch the train to Villabona. It was the last train until the weekend, and we had to keep to our schedule. Rene and Sofia would head back to her home in the mountains in the morning. She had been away for a long time, and there might be others waiting to leave France.

We collected our gear and walked away without turning around. Sofia told us it was bad luck to look back at friends when leaving, so we resisted the temptation to have one last look at them.

Chin up! I told myself.

We crossed the square, and church bells bid us away. We turned and saluted since we knew the priest was pulling the bell rope and watching us.

The train arrived, and we jumped aboard and found comfortable seats. The journey was about sixty miles, but with many stops to pick up others on their journeys, we would be lucky to arrive before dawn.

The train passed through some of the most beautiful country I'd ever seen. We were partially in the Basque region. As the train tracks wove in and around the hillsides, it was hard to imagine there was strife anywhere in the world.

Just when we were enjoying peace and quiet after many hours of starting and stopping, our train came to an abrupt halt. The screeching metal wheels against iron tracks sent sparks upward and into open windows.

The conductors passed word along that the track up ahead had been destroyed, most likely sabotaged by Spanish insurgents. Even though Spain was officially neutral, President Franco had been allowing German and Italian ships to use Spanish harbors and ports, an unpopular position held by many fighting against the European Axis.

We were told that buses were on their way from Villabona to transport us to San Sebastian. I learned that most of the train tracks along the coastal border of Spain, had been targeted sporadically, which required a quick change of our modus operandi.

Since my goal all along had been to get to Gibraltar, I had to figure out how to find a more interior route to Madrid. "Good grief. Will this shit ever end for me?" I exclaimed in total frustration.

Armand nodded at me, put his arm around my shoulder, and soothingly said, "Mon ami, you will have many stories to tell your grandchildren about this adventure!"

The buses arrived, and Armand and I said our goodbyes. He would take the bus to the coast, and his life would be that of a fisherman until the war was over. I, on the other hand, still had miles to go before I'd be on my way back to Britain to face whatever surprises were in store for me. I headed to the bus station and looked for some good advice. Instead, I found a Catholic church. *What else is new?*

As luck would have it, I learned that traveling south to Madrid and following trains and buses to Gibraltar was my only option. Little or no sabotage was being carried out in the interior of Spain. An additional six hundred kilometers through southern Spain would put me at the tip of Gibraltar. *These clergymen certainly have their fingers on the pulse of activity!*

The only way out for me, once I got there, would be air travel since there was a major escalation of the Allied forces gathered in the Atlantic. It appeared as though a major confrontation was about to happen off the coast of France.

I can only hope that I'll be on my way back to Britain before all hell breaks loose here.

CHAPTER 28

BLUE ATLANTIC

June 1944

The bus ride to Madrid was uneventful. Most passengers appeared to be families traveling together with children and baskets of food. In all the commotion, I realized I was hungry and had no food. I consoled myself by thinking that I could supply myself with food at a market in Madrid.

A dear little dark-eyed girl kept playing peekaboo with me and giggling. Her mother secured her in a seat and spread bread and cheese on a cloth on her lap. It smelled wonderful. The whole family was eating and drinking wine out of a wine bladder while they talked and laughed.

I rested my head against the seat and tried to sleep. I felt a nudge on my knee and looked up to see the child's mother. She offered me fruit, bread, and cheese, and she insisted that I partake in the offering. I thanked her in English, and she looked puzzled. It seemed as though she had me pegged as a local.

She pointed at me, turned to her family, and said, "Yankee *Americano*." *Good job*, I thought.

A resounding cheer came from everyone on the bus.

I felt tears burning my eyes, and my chest swelled with pride.

Wine was soon flowing and offered to me. As I drank voraciously, I hoped there were no Romany Gypsies on the bus. *Rene would be pissed!*

In Madrid, the bus dropped me at the train station. I bought a ticket to Seville. Since the train would leave in an hour, I had time to buy food at the outdoor market. I filled a basket with local delicacies to munch on during the trip.

I headed to the train with my gear and provisions and settled into a comfortable seat for the 230-kilometer trip.

The click-clack of the tracks sounded like a metronome pulsing the past few months through my brain. *I was shot down in March 1944, and so many things have brought me to this place and time: June 1, 1944. Some might say it's a lifetime, but it's a drop in the bucket in the grand scheme of things.*

I realized that my fatigue was overwhelming. It was unlike any tiredness I had ever felt. I gave in, and rest took over.

***

I woke to the loud train whistle announcing our arrival in Seville. Bustling passengers gathered belongings and exited onto the platform.

As far as I could tell, the next train was leaving any minute. I rushed to the ticket counter to buy my next ticket, which would take me to the Strait of Gibraltar. *I hope I find an airstrip somewhere between the Atlantic and the Mediterranean Sea. If not, I am screwed!* I found a seat and readied myself for the last leg of my journey.

We pulled out of the station and into oncoming darkness. I filled my belly with food and wine. *After all, I'm not driving.*

***

The train whistle woke me up as the sun was coming up somewhere over the Mediterranean. *What a beautiful sight!*

I watched the sunrise and thought about how to find a British plane on the coast of Spain at dawn, going in my direction, that would not require me to buy a ticket. My funds were low.

The war gods were with me! As I exited the train, the unmistakable sound of aircraft propellers and the smell of aviation fuel filled my heart with glee.

I walked to the end of the platform, and lo and behold, I saw a British version of an American C-47, a Dakota Skytrain, with my name all over it! *Holy shit!*

People milled around while a ramp was rolled out for passengers. Next thing I knew, a young officer approached me and said, "Are you Lieutenant Earle Carlow? We have been expecting you. Follow me."

I walked up the ramp and took a seat like I knew what I was doing. Inside the plane, the seats were lined on the sides of the aircraft. It was no-frills flying, but I would have been happy in the baggage compartment.

Once the boarding ramp was removed and the twin engines were whirling, the runway disappeared behind me. We went up and over the Strait of Gibraltar and far out over the Atlantic Ocean. I pinched myself to make sure I was not hallucinating.

The sound in the plane was deafening, and conversation was kept to a minimum. There were only men on the plane, and I learned that we all had escaped through the Pyrenees with help from the French Underground. *What stories we have to tell!*

CHAPTER 29

BLUE OCEANS MERGING

We climbed quickly over the Mediterranean, toward the east, and veered right.

We continued west, out over the Atlantic Ocean, and the pilot announced that it was the last flight out of that region for a while. He added, "Allied forces are advancing in the direction of Normandy, and thousands of ships that carry heavy equipment and troops have advanced toward the coast of France. We are flying far out over the Atlantic to avoid any confrontations with Axis forces that are patrolling beaches in France."

Maybe this is the beginning of the end of World War II. We all knew how lucky we were to have made it out of Europe when we did.

The C-47 approached the southern coast of Britain and the white cliffs of Dover. Onward and up, over the Thames and onto Debden, my base.

What will be waiting for me there? At this point, who bloody well knows? I might even be court-martialed for losing a bloody plane! If it's not enough that I won't receive any pay during my absence, I might even be thrown into the brig!

We landed in the fog on the turf runway at Debden, and darkness and fog enveloped us. Clamoring from the officers' club—at such a late hour—drowned out the aircraft noise.

As we descended the ramp, my mates chanted, "Kosky, you are back. You lazy bastard, we knew the Germans couldn't kill you!"

Nice to be called my old nickname again, I thought. I was swept up on their shoulders, carried into the officers' club, and immersed in the familiar smells of stale cigarette smoke, beer, and leather chairs. Camaraderie in chaos was all we needed to continue the brotherhood of war!

However, before any great welcoming party could begin, my commanding officer, Colonel Russell, tapped my shoulder. "Follow me, Captain Carlow!"

As I turned to address him, he pinned silver tracks on my shoulder, denoting my promotion to captain.

"Wow, what a welcome, sir!" I popped a salute and made direct eye contact with my superior.

"Intelligence people are on my ass about you and your little excursion through France and Spain! So, let's give them an earful and get on with the important stuff. I want to be the first to buy you a drink at the club—so suffer through the debriefing while it is all fresh in there!"

"Yes, sir." I followed him to the Quonset hut next to the mess hall.

The debriefing lasted a few hours. My written deposition would be given to military intelligence officers and locked away for safekeeping to protect the identities of my friends in the church and the French Underground.

As I feared, my flying career in the Air Force was over. If I was captured again, my knowledge of the inner sanctum of the Resistance movement could be a real asset to the Nazi cause. I would put my gun to my brain before incriminating any of my friends.

Finally, my debriefing was at an end. "Thank you for your service, Captain Carlow, and welcome back!"

I was whisked away to the bar, and the drinks flowed as war stories were shared. The quiet ones didn't share; our stories were too personal.

The boisterous airmen bragged about kills and conquests that were too numerous to be believed. They—at least in their memories—were invincible. I finally begged off and returned to my BOQ, which looked the same as I had left it: tidy and with bed made and fresh laundry stowed in cupboard.

I was bone weary with every possible ache and pain imaginable running through my body—even my teeth and armpits hurt! I collapsed into my bunk. *Tomorrow is another day. I can hardly wait!*

CHAPTER 30

BRITISH BLUES

June 6, 1944

Chaos reigned over the coast of France. Allied forces met head-on with Germany, and it was hell!

The British people had endured their own special hell on earth and lost family members to combat duty and bombing attacks endured at home.

I had lost at least twenty-five pounds in the past four months, and I was plagued with insomnia and nightmares. No matter. I was assigned to the Fourth Fighter Group Headquarters in Debden and had to put my personal stress behind me.

With a dozen other officers, I watched the devastation being revealed on the world map. Our job was to monitor fleets of ships all over the Atlantic and track their positions by using pointers to advance them into new locations closer to coastal France. We passed on this information to our superiors, and they transmitted data by radio and Morse code to ground troops, air support, and naval operations.

After seven months of constant decision-making and literally no time off, I was almost fried. The war was coming to an end.

The Battle of the Bulge in December 1944 was the historical defining end of World War II. I was now a card-carrying civilian. *Hallelujah!*

I had not received any mail from my friends in London concerning the safety of the Ceadel family in Tottenham. No news of a baby having been born around this time. I asked for some leave to check things out for myself, and it was granted.

Trains going into London were back on a regular schedule. I caught a ride into the city and took the bus to Tottenham—the last known address of the Ceadel family. The bus stopped at the top of West Green Road, but it could not access Blackboy Lane.

I could see why: all the brick row houses were nothing more than rubble. The buzz bombs had done their job well. Some of the iron fence posts still stood in front of what used to be people's homes and front gates. I walked down the broken sidewalk, counted sixty iron posts, and came to 60 Blackboy Lane—her family's home. *No house left? What to do!*

I caught the bus back to the far end of West Green and found our favorite café. Marg and Kath, our longtime friends, were still inside.

Marg was cooking eggs and sausages at the grill, and Kath was drinking tea at the counter in her ambulance uniform. It was just like old times when Hilda and I used to go there for meals.

I stood there not knowing what to say.

"What'll you have, mate?" Margaret asked without turning around.

I cleared my throat.

As she turned around, she exclaimed, "Blimey all to hell! It's bloody well the disappearing Yank."

Through the tears burning my eyes, I saw her jump over the counter to give me a big kiss and hug.

Kath was quiet.

"Good to see you too, mate!" I choked out.

The three of us made small talk briefly.

This is going to be a tough conversation. "Just came back from 60—give me all the news."

The looks on their faces told me everything—well, almost everything.

In a very hushed voice, Marg said, "They were all in there when the bomb hit. I was here and had just fixed tea for Kath before she went off ambulance duty. We both raced down to see if anyone was alive anywhere. We found 60 right away ... by counting the fence posts. We picked our way through smoke, fires, and gushing water and saw the two of them huddled near the brick chimney. It looked like Hilda and her dad. We heard a baby crying and saw someone draped over a crib. We knew immediately that it was Hilda's mum. Ruby had lain over the crib when she heard the bombs screaming down. Her body kept the ceiling above from falling on the baby. She died in the process."

Kath picked up the gauntlet and added, "We took the baby back to Marg's cafe and fed her goat milk from the farm in Norfolk. She thrived on it. Who knew that you could give that to a baby? We had no choice!"

"I am humbled and feel like such a shithead that this responsibility fell to you both," I confessed.

"Well, she is now two months old, and her birth certificate says you are her father. Hilda's husband is back from Africa and wants nothing to do with anything. Now, mate, can you deal with what I am about to show you?" Marg asked.

"Of course … bring her to me." I swallowed a great lump in my throat.

She brought out a swaddled lump in a blanket and placed her in my arms. She was still and quiet.

Marg folded back the blanket to reveal a tiny baby with a shock of curly red hair. *Her mother's hair for sure.* The eyes opened suddenly. The intense blue eyes electrified me for a moment and told me we belonged to each other. *All I need to know!*

"I'll take her back to Debden with me. I'll be here for a few more years as an attaché to American intelligence on the base. I will care for her there. Does she have a name?"

Marg said, "Her birth certificate says Elizabeth Vera Carlow, but we call her Baby Libby. We have grown to love her. You bloody well take care of her—or there will be hell to pay!"

"I need a couple of days back at the base to arrange a house and a nurse, and then I will be back."

Marg and Kath looked at each other and agreed to the arrangement— if they could visit regularly.

When I left the café, I looked back, ignoring the old superstition to "never look back when you are leaving people you love."

I have a chance to make everything right.

CHAPTER 31

RED, WHITE, AND BLUE FUTURE

July 1946

The next few years passed quickly. My life in Debden with Libby was so happy, and I hired our dear Jane as Libby's nanny. Jane was a wonderful friend and surrogate mum to my toddler. As a nurse, Jane saw more than her share of action on the battlefield. Her need for a change and a simpler life led her to us. She and I were war-torn, kindred spirits and communicated reminders of our turbulent past to each other with fleeting glances. Our relationship never evolved into a romance, but we had a special bond nonetheless.

My time in Britain was coming to an end. Jane knew it and was ready to embrace her new role as head nurse at the Mayfair Clinic in London. I had plans to return to America and start over in a new career that was unrelated to flying. I had been offered a job with the postal service and thought it would suit me fine.

I contacted my brother Leo and his wife, Emm, about the adoption of Libby. They want a child desperately and have not been blessed. They agreed to fly to Britain and stay with us as we all get reacquainted. They will get to know Libby's two-year-old self before taking her back to Skowhegan. All the legal adoption papers will be done through the American consulate office on the base.

***

I had difficulty convincing myself that it was the right thing to do—even though I was repeating history in the same way my father had left me. I knew Libby would have a wonderful life with them. I was not the father I should have been at that point in my life. *Excuses are easy, and commitments are tough.*

The day had come. Emm had dressed Libby in a blue frock that matched her eyes! *Way to break my heart, Emm!* The tiny fingers clutched mine, and I hugged Libby close.

Libby said, "Bye, Bird." Those were first words she ever said to me. Apparently, I was Bird. *Who knew?*

They were gone. I would see them back in the States, but I would be Uncle Earle, and Leo and Emm would tell her this story someday.

CHAPTER 32

BLUE LIGHTNING OVER SAN ANTONIO

November 1960

The passengers were restless and tired of circling in the holding pattern over the approach to the airport in San Antonio. The pilot, on the intercom, kept everyone updated about severe thunderstorms in the area.

The plane jerked up and down as the turbulence tossed the aircraft in different directions. Lightning strikes bounced off the wings and caused the cabin lights to flicker.

Earle emerged from a deep sleep and became fully engaged in pilot mode. Quickly assessing the situation, he said, "Let's hope we don't get clobbered by a microburst! We need to find the ground and fast—before we run out of fuel!" He muttered under his breath, "Goddam Romany Gypsy woman was right. I'm going to die in a plane crash just as she said!"

Those were the last words Earle ever spoke.

The plane exploded in midair, and the 727 inverted itself. Stowed items flew everywhere. Passengers screamed, prayed, and begged for their lives. The chaotic scene was a nightmare. The reality of the horror scene was confirmed by lightning strikes that lit up the dark cabin.

Leo tried to comfort Libby and repeated, "It's going to be okay!"

The aircraft hit the runway with tremendous force, and bodies were flung everywhere.

Black smoke filled the cabin, and the plane finally came to a stop.

"Get on my back, Libby, and don't let go—no matter what happens!" Leo screamed above the bedlam.

He felt her death grip around his neck as he crawled toward the flames that shot over the top of the fuselage. They tumbled onto the tarmac and rolled away from the inferno. Panic-stricken passengers wandered around and looked for family as emergency crews ferried them to a triage area.

Leo and Libby found themselves in the terminal with only cuts and minor burns. Medical people were busy with iodine and bandages, and they assessed wounds and foreign bodies in cuts.

A nurse approached and asked, "What can I do to help you?"

Leo said, "I must go look for my brother. He was traveling with us. Can you come with me while I try to convince the emergency people to let me see the victims?"

Leo's request was granted, but Libby stayed in the terminal.

Body parts were strewn among the wreckage, fire trucks hosed down hot metal, and medics transported injured passengers into waiting ambulances. Body bags were lined up at the edge of the runway.

***

The nurse helped Leo as he began the grim task of opening the top sections of the body bags. After opening a few bags, Leo found the one that he did not want to see. He slowly returned to the terminal and cried uncontrollably as he wondered why this chance to finally build a relationship with his brother had been snatched away forever.

Libby sat quietly as Leo approached. She looked up and asked, "Did you find Bird? Where is he?"

Leo asked, "Who is Bird?"

She gave him a strange, faraway look and answered, "Earle is Bird."

Leo held Libby and sobbed. "My darling girl, he didn't survive the crash. I must tell you that Earle was your biological father."

Libby took a deep breath, looked at him with piercing blue eyes that were brimming with tears, and said, "I know, Dad."

Lightning Source UK Ltd.
Milton Keynes UK
UKHW010638100822
407113UK00001B/255